# Educating Eleanor

Also in the *X Libris* series:

# Educating Eleanor

## Nina Sheridan

**X**
LIBRIS

An *X Libris* Book

First published by X Libris in 1997

A CIP catalogue record for this book
is available from the British Library.

ISBN 0 7515 1929 4

Photoset in North Wales by
Derek Doyle & Associates, Mold, Clwyd
Printed and bound in Great Britain by
Clays Ltd, St Ives plc

X Libris
A Division of
Little, Brown and Company (UK)
Brettenham House
Lancaster Place
London WC2E 7EN

# Educating Eleanor

# Chapter One

---

'MICHAEL, YOU CAN'T honestly expect me to take this lying down? I put as much into that house as you did – more, in fact. If you want to keep it on, that's fine, but you'll have to buy me out. I want my half.'

Eleanor Dawes listened as her soon-to-be-ex husband proceeded to weave a predictable path from pleading to threats. Once upon a time, her stomach would have been churning by now and she would have acceded to his every demand, throwing in some extra concessions of her own for good measure. Now, though, she knew better and she let him burn himself out. When at last he fell silent again, she said calmly, 'My solicitor will be in touch with yours. Goodbye, Michael.' She placed the receiver quietly back onto its cradle.

The coffee she had made for herself just before the telephone rang had grown cold, so she went to make another. Michael had gone too far this time. The separation had already depleted her savings out of existence; if she didn't have a roof over her head in the form of this cottage she'd be virtually destitute.

Eleanor turned and smiled at the framed photograph of her grandmother which took pride of place on the shelf over the small dining table.

'You saved my life, leaving me the cottage, *Mam du*,' she said aloud.

A cat rubbed up against her lower legs and mewled plaintively.

'And you, Thomas,' she said, sweeping the black ball of fur up with one hand. 'Whatever would I do without you and Dylan to talk to?'

Dylan, the fat tabby who rarely budged from the best armchair, raised a lazy eyelid as she paused to stroke him en route to the sofa in front of the TV. *Pebble Mill* was starting and Eleanor settled back with her coffee and Thomas on her lap to watch.

Watching lunchtime television was Eleanor's way of breaking up her day when she was at work on a book. Today, she had the added satisfaction of having typed '*end*' on the last page of her manuscript. She refused to think about what she would do next, determinedly basking in the glow of a project completed. Normally, her agent would have already negotiated her a new deal so that she could start on the next book almost as soon as she finished the last, but what with the public scandal which erupted around Michael after he lost the by-election, and the upheaval of moving from London to South-West Wales, Eleanor hadn't managed to work out a new proposal.

It was a miracle she had been able to complete this book, she reflected grimly; her concentration had been sorely affected by the problems in her personal life. Unfortunately, she needed the income from her writing now more than ever, and if she didn't obtain a new commission soon she was going to have to find some other way of keeping body and soul together.

She sighed, only half watching the television as her mind went over the unpaid bills in the drawer of the bureau in the corner of the room. Living rent-free was a huge help, but there were other day-to-day expenses to be covered.

The television presenter introduced his first guest and Eleanor turned her attention to the screen. Her lip curled as she saw the man walking down the steps to join the presenter on the sofa.

He was tall with dark, wavy hair which had a habit of flopping over one eye in such a contrived fashion that Eleanor could imagine him blow-drying it to fall just that way. He was lean and fit-looking, his black jeans moulding the contours of his long thighs, his boots polished so that they shone dully under the studio lights. His mid-blue silk shirt was open at the neck, just enough to give the viewer a glimpse of curly black chest hair at his throat, but not enough for it to look as though a medallion belonged there. As he sat down, he tucked his black jacket back so that it didn't obscure the sight of his trim waist and neat black suede belt.

Marcus Grant had been attracting a great deal of publicity just lately. An American sexologist, he was famous for his ground-breaking research into sexual response and erotic potential. His subject matter, coupled with his smouldering, film-star looks, made him a media dream. Eleanor hated him, instinctively.

'Surely,' the interviewer was saying to him now, 'sexual desire is an emotion which some people experience more often than others?'

Marcus Grant leaned forward in his seat, his dark eyes like two liquid pools, inviting his audience to drown in them.

'On the contrary, Alan,' he replied, his voice like smooth Guinness, trickling over the senses. 'Although the initial experience of arousal can be said to be instinctive, the frequency, and the intensity with which it is felt, is a learned response.'

'So, are you saying that we can all learn to become more sexual animals?' the presenter asked, raising his eyebrows knowingly at the camera.

Marcus Grant looked straight into the camera lens so that Eleanor, and, no doubt, half the female viewers in the country, felt he was talking directly to her.

4

'Absolutely. I meet so many people – women in particular – who write themselves off as frigid when, in fact, with a little training and practice they could discover a whole new world of pleasure.'

Eleanor pointed the remote control at the television and erased Marcus Grant's face from the screen.

'Smug git!' she said aloud.

Feeling intensely uncomfortable, Eleanor decided she would take herself off for a brisk walk down to the post office where she could post her manuscript.

Upstairs in the small bedroom, she stripped off the baggy old tracksuit she wore at the word processor and pulled out clean jeans and a cotton jumper to wear over a T-shirt. Catching a glimpse of herself in the dressing-table mirror, she paused, her eyes assessing.

Her body hadn't changed much in the last ten years. At thirty she was still slender, still firm-breasted, and her bottom hadn't yet succumbed to gravity. Pulling her clothes on over her serviceable M&S undies, Eleanor thought with impatience of what the American had said. Michael had always said she was frigid. The truth was, she simply didn't have a very high sex-drive.

It had bothered her, when she was younger and her contemporaries had spent half their time at college getting laid. Now though, she was comfortable with herself and she doubted if, at this stage in her life, she was likely to change. Learned response indeed! Marcus Grant made women sound like performing monkeys, talking about *training* and *practice*. Eleanor guessed that it probably didn't occur to him that many women, like herself, were perfectly happy with the sexual drive they had been given, thank you very much!

The telephone was ringing as she ran down the stairs.

'Gloria!' she said as she recognised her agent's voice. 'How are you?'

'Fine. More to the point, how are *you*, stuck in that godforsaken place?'

Eleanor laughed, for she could almost hear the shudder in Gloria's voice.

'It is *not* a godforsaken place, Gloria,' she said patiently, knowing that she was wasting her breath. Anything outside the capital was the back of beyond to Gloria. 'It's more like God's promised land. You'll have to come and spend a weekend in the summer, and I guarantee you'll fall in love with it yourself.'

'That's very kind of you,' Gloria replied with heavy irony. 'Actually, I was ringing you about a job, not to discuss the merits of sheep versus cars. Have you finished the book?'

'I'm just about to post it.'

'Good. Have you ever heard of Marcus Grant?'

Eleanor sucked in her breath.

'Funnily enough, I've just been watching him on *Pebble Mill*.'

'*Pebble Mill*?' Gloria repeated, mystified.

Realising that her agent probably didn't even know there *was* such a thing as daytime television, let alone watch it, Eleanor changed the subject.

'What about him?'

'He's gorgeous, isn't he?'

'Hmm,' Eleanor said non-committally. 'So what about him?'

'He needs a co-author for his next book, *Becoming Sexual*. Naff title, but a sure-fire bestseller. Knowing you're free, I put your name forward and he wants to meet you.'

'What! You've already talked to him about me?'

'He knows and admires your work, and he's offering a good deal.'

Gloria mentioned an advance that made Eleanor's eyes water. If she took this assignment, she would be financially secure for the next twelve months. Could she bring herself to work closely with a man whom she loathed on sight?

'I'm not interested, Gloria.'

'What? Why not?'

'The subject doesn't appeal.'

'Oh, come on, Eleanor! At least meet the guy and see what he's got in mind. I know you're feeling a bit raw, after what happened with Michael, but this might be just the thing to take your mind off it. And I know you need the money . . .' she wheedled.

'Sorry, Gloria, but I won't do it. I have a feeling that Mr Grant and I just would not get on.'

'What makes you think that?' Gloria asked, clearly surprised.

'Only that he's the epitome of everything I hate in a man.'

'Explain.'

'Okay. For starters, he comes across as arrogant, overbearing and self-regarding. He obviously considers himself God's gift to womankind, and I object to any man who sets himself up as an expert on female sexuality. Is that enough for you?'

'I see. And you've surmised all this from watching him on the television?'

Eleanor felt herself flush.

'I've read interviews too,' she defended herself, somewhat lamely. 'Come on, Gloria – the way he talks about women, he can't be anything but an arrogant bastard, at best.'

'Point taken,' Gloria conceded. 'You've got to admit, he's got a cute bum, though.'

'Gloria!' Eleanor laughed in spite of herself. 'No. N-O. All right?'

'I'll leave you to think it over and ring you in the morning. Ciao for now!'

She rang off, leaving Eleanor feeling exasperated. She might be broke, but there was no way she was going to put her name to a book which encouraged women to 'train' their sexual responses!

Once she had delivered her manuscript to the post office and gossiped a while with the post mistress, Eleanor decided to take a walk along the beach. Spring was in the air and, although this part of Wales never became overcrowded even in the high season, now the beach was virtually deserted.

Though moving to Wales had been a necessity rather than a choice, Eleanor was glad she had come. The local people, whether out of affection for her grandma, or out of a natural antipathy to the Tories, had welcomed her into their homes and made her feel as though she really belonged. As English as she was, Eleanor was very aware of the honour that had been granted her and she was determined not to taint her new neighbours with the scandal she hoped to leave behind her in London.

As she walked along the firm-sanded beach, Eleanor's mind began to clear and she turned her thoughts to the proposition Gloria had put to her. It was true that she had made a name for herself as the author of several popular, accessible books about modern medical matters. She had discovered a knack for presenting often quite complicated medical research in an easily read style which meant she was often asked to contribute to magazines and television documentaries. Women in particular seemed to appreciate her straight-talking, unpatronising approach and, if it wasn't for Michael's avarice, she would be living quite comfortably on what she earned.

9

Her face clouded as she thought about Michael. He had been so passionately idealistic when she had first met him. Sweeping her along on the tide of his ambition, she'd stood by his side as he worked his way up in the party, finally being elected to the Commons. From whence he proceeded to destroy himself, dragging Eleanor down with him.

'You're looking very pensive, *cariad*.'

Eleanor almost jumped out of her skin as the deep, lilting voice sounded close to her ear.

'Rhys!' she laughed. 'I didn't hear your footsteps on the sand.'

'You were so deep in thought I doubt if you'd have heard me if I'd been walking on gravel!' he said. 'Come and have a cup of tea with me at Mrs Williams's place.'

Smiling, Eleanor tucked her hand comfortably in the crook of Rhys's arm and walked with him towards the steps leading up to the roadway. His arm felt strong and steady and dependable and Eleanor was surprised to realise how pleased she was to see him.

'No work today?' she asked him, eyeing his ragged jeans and the baggy, shapeless sweatshirt he wore.

'I'm playing hookey,' he told her. 'Actually, I wanted to see you.'

'Me?'

'Yes. I was thinking that you'd be needing the services of a good lawyer if the story in today's

*Mirror* is true.'

Eleanor frowned.

'I haven't seen any newspapers today,' she admitted.

Sensing Rhys's discomfort, Eleanor steeled herself for the worst.

'Here,' he said, pulling the folded tabloid out of his back pocket. 'You'd better read it yourself.'

Eleanor sat on the edge of the sea wall and opened the paper at the page Rhys indicated. Michael smiled back at her from a wedding photograph, a younger, more trusting version of herself on his arm.

'Oh no!' she whispered.

*Tory Wife Drove MP to Suicide Attempt* ran the headline. *The Truth surrounding Michael Dawes' Sham Marriage*.

Eleanor felt sick. Folding the newspaper, she handed it back to Rhys and covered her face with her hands. After a moment, she felt his touch, tentative on her shoulder.

'You could sue for libel, El. You've suffered enough without them blackening your name like this.'

Eleanor looked up into his handsome face, so full of concern for her, and struggled to smile. She had known Rhys Jones since they were both in nappies – his family had lived across the street from her grandmother and the two of them had been inseparable during every summer of their childhood. She could still catch an occasional glimpse of the tow-headed, freckled-faced boy in the man sitting beside her now. Only now his hair was blond, his face interesting rather than cute, handsome but with the same unusual light-blue eyes which seemed to see everything.

Rhys had been the object of her first crush, they had shared their first kiss, their first date and their friendship had endured over the years so that Eleanor knew that Rhys was the one person in all the world on whom she could rely. He was always there with a word of encouragement, a smile, a hug, and now he was offering himself in a professional capacity.

'I don't want to sue, Rhys,' she told him now. 'It would only prolong the unpleasantness. You know, Michael actually had the nerve to ring me this morning to harangue me about the house. He must have been disappointed by my lack of reaction!' She laughed bitterly.

'I am going to need a good divorce lawyer though – do you think your colleague Amy would represent me?'

Rhys nodded.

'Of course. But I would strongly advise you to issue a restraining order on this kind of thing – scum like this shouldn't be allowed to get away with it!'

Eleanor appreciated the outrage expressed on her behalf, but still she shook her head.

'It will be Duncan who's behind all this. If I sue I'll be playing straight into his hands.'

Rhys regarded her thoughtfully for a few moments.

'Why are they doing this to you, Eleanor? I can't understand it.'

Eleanor shrugged wearily.

'I get the impression that Michael blames me for having to resign. And I suppose he has a point – I was responsible, at least indirectly, for his affair becoming public knowledge. So far I've had all the public sympathy. He and Duncan think I should sign the house over to Michael as some kind of compensation for his career going down the tubes.'

'What kind of warped reasoning is that?'

Eleanor smiled at him, both amused and warmed by his vehemence.

'As you say, it's warped. But there doesn't seem to be a lot I can do about it. It's not as if I have a public position, so they can't really harm my career. Spreading nasty rumours about me isn't going to get them anywhere – sticks and stones and all that. I prefer to ignore it.'

'And hope they'll go away?'

'Perhaps.'

Rhys sighed, his large, warm hand reaching for hers and enclosing it.

'All right,' he said. 'Come on – I'll walk you home.'

'What happened to that cup of tea you promised me?' she protested half-heartedly.

Rhys's eyes scanned her face and she sensed

13

that she had grown pale.

'You can make us one at home,' he told her and they walked back to the cottage in companionable silence.

Waiting for the kettle to boil in her tiny kitchen, Eleanor could see Rhys through the open door, sprawled in an armchair with Thomas on his lap. Dylan eyed him disdainfully, but then even he leapt up onto his knee after a few minutes. Rhys had that effect on women as well as cats, she mused to herself – no one could resist him for long. And yet Rhys had remained steadfastedly single, content, it seemed, with his lot.

He smiled at her now as she handed him a mug of tea. He had the kind of smile that lit up his light-blue eyes from within, making them twinkle sexily.

'Why have you never married, Rhys?' she asked him as she sat opposite with her own steaming mug.

'You know I'm waiting for you, El,' he replied. He smiled as he said it, but Eleanor was aware that the smile didn't quite reach his eyes.

'You deserve better than me, Rhys,' she said quietly. 'What happened to that girl Sara you were serious about?'

'She couldn't measure up. Why are you always doing yourself down, *cariad*?'

Eleanor shifted uncomfortably in her chair. Normally she avoided intimate chats with the attractive man who was now regarding her so seriously, but, despite her protestations that she ignored such things, the malicious newspaper article had caught her with her defences down.

'It never was very good between Michael and me, you know,' she said softly.

Rhys made an impatient sound at the back of his throat.

'Hardly surprising when you consider his secret.'

Eleanor shook his head.

'Michael wasn't homosexual before he met me.'

Rhys regarded her with amazement.

'Is that what he told you? Eleanor – think about what you're saying. It's not your fault. None of it is your fault.'

'I know that in here,' she agreed, tapping the side of her head. 'But I can't help but wonder, if I'd been better at . . . at the intimate side of our marriage, maybe he'd not have looked elsewhere.'

Rhys put down his mug and came to kneel on the floor in front of her. Eleanor knew that, for his sake, she ought to move away, but something kept her still. His touch, as he reached out to smooth her long hair away from her face, was gentle, full of tenderness. Eleanor felt a tightening in her throat, an unwelcome stirring in response to his nearness. She could feel the warmth of his body even from this distance, could smell the clean, salty tang of his skin. It made her feel dizzy and weak and she pulled herself together with an effort.

'You're a good friend to me, Rhys,' she said, a

slight quiver in her voice betraying the effect he was having on her.

Rhys grimaced and allowed his hand to drop to his side.

'But nothing more,' he added, his voice flat and expressionless.

'Does there have to be more?' Eleanor asked him, her eyes pleading. What on earth had possessed her to allow this conversation to develop? 'I value your friendship.'

'As I do yours. But I have to ask you, Eleanor – is there really no chance for me with you? Would you never consider marrying me?'

Eleanor felt her heart constrict. She had sensed this question brewing ever since she'd come home to Wales and she had been dreading it. She was fond of Rhys, loved him even, as a sister loves a brother, but she couldn't give him what she knew he wanted. She had a feeling that he would settle for less, but she thought too much of him to offer anything less than he deserved. Picking her words carefully, she sought to turn him down without jeopardising the friendship she valued so highly.

'Rhys, if there was any chance of my marrying again, believe me, it could only be you. But there isn't any chance. I'm happy on my own.'

'You weren't destined to be alone, Eleanor. You're far too sensual a woman to be content to lead a celibate life.'

Eleanor shook her head.

'Life is a lot less complicated without sex,' she told him.

'You're wrong, Eleanor. Just because it wasn't good between you and Michael doesn't mean it could never be good at all.'

Eleanor shook her head.

'Rhys—'

She gasped as suddenly, without warning, he pulled her into his arms and kissed her. At first she was too surprised to respond, then she felt the warmth of his lips moving over hers, coaxing them apart, and she knew that she didn't love him as a sister does a brother at all. There was nothing in the least bit filial in the way her head swam and her body responded to the sweet, curiously familiar taste of him. It was good, so good, and she wanted it to go on.

She gazed at him, wide-eyed, as he broke away.

'Something for you to think about, Ellie,' he said, a note of bitterness in his voice that wounded her.

'It was just a kiss, Rhys,' she protested.

He seemed to be about to say something, then his shoulders sagged and he dropped his eyes from hers. With a sigh, Rhys stood up. He looked down on her for several minutes. 'I'd best be off,' he said, regret colouring his tone. 'I'll tell Amy you'll be coming into Carmarthen to see her. Try not to worry too much, Eleanor – these things have a way of working themselves out.'

Eleanor had the feeling that he was talking

17

about himself as much as her battle with Michael and she smiled sadly. If only he could meet someone else, some loving girl who would make him happy – nothing would give her more pleasure. She frowned as her heart gave a little somersault at the thought. The sensation was far from pleasurable.

'Goodbye, Rhys,' she said softly, closing the door behind him.

It hurt her to think that she had disappointed him again. The image of his crestfallen face stayed with her. She refused to think about the kiss, and how it had shaken her. Perhaps it would be easier for him if she went away for a few days. The divorce was going to be expensive and Gloria had offered her a way to solve both problems. It struck her as ironic that she was even considering working with Marcus Grant, but the idea was looking more appealing by the minute.

Gloria was ecstatic to hear from her again so soon.

'I thought that maybe a confirmed celibate might be able to give a new slant to a book called *Becoming Sexual*,' Eleanor told her wryly.

Gloria snorted.

'I doubt you'll want to stay that way for long once you meet the delicious Mr Grant,' she told her. 'He called by the office less than an hour ago – he's very keen to meet you.'

'Really?' Eleanor was unimpressed. 'Well, it can't do any harm for us to meet. We might hate each other on sight anyway.'

'I doubt it,' Gloria said pointedly. She proceeded to give Eleanor details of Marcus Grant's
hotel and promised to ring her when she had set
up a meeting.

Later that night, Eleanor lay in bed, unable to
sleep. Rhys had telephoned to see that she was all
right and the memory of his dear, familiar voice
still warmed her. Gloria had confirmed that she
was to meet Marcus Grant at three the following
day and she had set the alarm so that she could be
up to catch the early train.

Her whole body felt prickly and no matter what
position she took up, she could not make herself
comfortable. She began to stroke her arms,
comforting herself, enjoying the warm slip of her
palms over her skin. They were inconvenient,
these occasional bouts of sexual tension, but they
were easily assuaged by a little gentle masturbation. Sex with oneself was so much less
stressful without the fear of disappointing a
partner.

Closing her eyes, Eleanor imagined that they
were Rhys's hands smoothing and stroking her
skin, edging their way down over her stomach to
the silky-soft skin of her inner thighs. The tender,
sensitive flesh between them was moist and
warm and she sighed as her fingers fluttered
across the delicate folds.

From the limited experience she had had with

19

Rhys before, she knew that he would be a gentle, unselfish lover. She imagined him now burying his face between her breasts, kissing the skin and sucking the burgeoning nubs into the hot, wet cavity of his mouth.

Her breasts hardened and crested as she thought of it, her legs sliding apart on the cool cotton sheets, her labia opening. With the middle finger of her right hand she traced the slippery channels of flesh, teasing herself until she could bear the suspense no longer.

Her clitoris was a hard, smooth promontory which hardened still more under her fingers. Eleanor found her breath catching in her chest as she rubbed it, manipulating all the little nerve endings until they quivered with life.

She imagined Rhys closing his lips over the little nub, worrying at it with his tongue and his teeth, and she felt the tension build, moving inexorably towards climax. Once she had passed the point of no return, once her body was slick with sweat and her breathing was rapid and harsh, she pushed herself on, reaching for that moment of altered consciousness, the release which her body craved.

Eleanor lost control of her mind just before she lost control of her body. Instead of seeing Rhys pleasuring her with his fingers and his tongue, a sudden, harsher image forced its way into her head, of Michael as she had seen him that fateful afternoon, ploughing into the body of Duncan,

20

his private secretary. Even as her mind recoiled, her body made the jump into orgasm and she came with a sob, closing her legs on her own hand and curling up into a ball.

Tears of shame sprang to her eyes as she acknowledged that, once again, the image of her husband and his lover had acted as a trigger to her own orgasm. How could she find something which so appalled her so unbearably arousing?

If Rhys could see into her mind, *then* he would understand why she couldn't make him happy. He'd recoil from the truth, his image of her forever tarnished by the knowledge of her darkest fantasies.

She jumped as the telephone rang, fumbling for the receiver in the semi-darkness.

'Hello?' she said, aware that her voice was smoky with spent passion.

There was a deep chuckle at the other end of the line.

'You sound as though you've been having a good time,' a voice which was strangely familiar said.

'Who is this?' Eleanor said, embarrassment and guilt making her sharp. She sat up in the bed, pulling the covers around her protectively.

'You don't know me, Mrs Dawes, but I believe we are to meet tomorrow afternoon. My name is Grant. Marcus Grant.'

*Of course it is*, Eleanor thought angrily. Who else would be arrogant enough to call a stranger at this time of night?

'Do you know what time it is?' she said icily.

'It's just after eleven. I'm sorry – did I wake you?'

He sounded genuinely surprised and Eleanor softened a little.

'I always go to bed early,' she said.

'Oh. Well, I hope you won't be too averse to a few late nights when we begin work,' he said.

'Mr Grant, we haven't even agreed on a contract yet,' Eleanor reminded him coolly. 'Was there a reason for your call?'

'Of course. I was hoping to put back our appointment to four rather than three. Would that be convenient?'

'Yes, that would be fine.'

'Good. I'll leave you to get back to what you were doing . . . Eleanor,' he said with a casual insolence that took Eleanor's breath away. She was about to tell him to mind his own business, but she realised that he had already replaced the telephone.

Lying back on the pillows, Eleanor stared up at the darkened ceiling. Why did he have to phone her at that moment, of all times? She groaned inwardly. He can't have *known*, she told herself rationally. Yet he had known, she could tell by the timbre of his voice as much as by his words.

Perhaps she should call the meeting off altogether – it was obvious they weren't going to get along. Then she thought of Rhys and her empty bank account, and she knew that turning down this assignment would be tantamount to both emotional and financial suicide.

She'd meet with Marcus Grant tomorrow, she decided, and she'd interview him as carefully as he would no doubt interview her. And she would make it perfectly clear to him that she considered the assignment to be purely professional, that innuendos such as those he had uttered on the telephone were strictly off-limits.

That decided, she settled down into the bed and closed her eyes. But it was a long, long time before she fell asleep.

# Chapter Two

*THE GRIMY, RAIN-WASHED* streets of London came as a shock to Eleanor as she stepped off the train at Paddington. After the lush, green peace of Pembrokeshire the city seemed to exist on one discordant screech of sound which hurt her ears and made her feel disorientated.

Strange, how quickly she had adapted to her new home, she thought as she allowed herself to be swept along by a tide of commuters towards the taxi rank. The hotel was easily reached by Tube, but Eleanor felt she simply couldn't face the idea of battling her way to the right platform before squashing herself into an airless carriage with countless strangers.

Sitting back in the relative comfort of a black cab, she gazed out of the window at the people rushing by and recalled how she had once been one of them, among them, always in a rush. Now her life was so much gentler, the pace much more conducive to writing. Sometimes, at home, she wondered if she missed the metropolitan life. Now she knew that she did not, and she relaxed into her seat with the smile of someone glad to be a mere visitor.

It wasn't strictly necessary to go straight to the hotel since she wasn't due to meet Marcus Grant until four, but Gloria had booked her a room so that she could stay overnight and Eleanor had requested that a copy of Grant's latest book be left at reception for her. After the long journey, she intended to have lunch courtesy of room service while she read it.

The hotel was a surprise. From what she had seen and heard of Marcus Grant, she expected him to have chosen somewhere modern and efficient, but essentially soulless. Instead she found herself deposited outside the dignified façade of a tall Edwardian terrace, guarded by an elderly doorman in full dress uniform.

'Allow me to carry your bag, madam,' he said at once, walking unhurriedly down the steps to greet her.

His smile was cool and professional and Eleanor agreed with a gracious nod. Inside, the foyer was lit by a single enormous glass chandelier embellished with countless crystal droplets which tinkled discreetly as the door opened and closed.

The man who checked her in was as stiff as the

doorman and Eleanor found herself responding to the porter's cheery grin far more warmly than she might otherwise have thought was wise.

After the formality of her greeting, Eleanor's room came as another surprise. Tastefully decorated in shades of pink and soft dove grey, it was furnished in sumptuous style with well cared-for antique furniture. The room was dominated by a huge brass bed, the head and foot boards of which were wrought of the most elaborate ironwork. The bedspread was of faded pink satin and was piled with cushions of various shapes, sizes and fabrics. It looked so inviting that, ignoring the small desk by the window, Eleanor kicked off her shoes and made herself comfortable.

Grant's book was called *Women's Secret Lives*. There was a brief biography of the author on the back flap of the jacket, listing his academic credentials and repeating praise for his work by obscure journals, the pedigree of which Eleanor didn't trust. There was a small, black and white photograph of him staring moodily into the camera. Eleanor could feel the smoulder emanating from the page.

Given her own ambivalence about sex, Eleanor found the subject-matter intensely uncomfortable. The book began with a treatise on the potential in women to develop a rich fantasy-life, sometimes at the expense, so the author suggested, of their own long-term relationships.

The following chapters described, in quite toe-curling detail, the fantasies that various women had allegedly described to Marcus Grant for the sake of his research. The thought of divulging her most intimate thoughts to a man like Grant, as these women apparently had done, made Eleanor feel quite ill.

Her eyes widened as she read of women who fantasised about things Eleanor had never dreamed could be conducive to sexual pleasure. Doggedly reading every word in the interest of being fully informed about Grant's work when she met him, Eleanor soon became aware that, whilst her conscious mind was often repelled by the acts described, her body was actually responding.

One scenario in particular caught her imagination. The woman telling the story was introduced as 'Jennifer', a suburban American housewife in her thirties, happily married with what she described as a 'normal' sex life and two school-age children. The story was told verbatim.

'My favourite fantasy starts with my husband coming home after work one night with new clothes for me in a carrier bag. Now, my man *never* buys me clothes, I doubt he even knows what size I take, y'know? So this is like, real fantasy territory, right from the start!

Anyways, he tells me he's arranged for an overnight babysitter and that he's taking me somewhere real special – somewhere I've never been before. Now, I don't say too much, don't ask too many questions cos I don't want him to go changing his mind. So I run me a bath and afterwards I rub perfumed cream into my skin so that it's all soft and sweet-smelling, then I go over to the bed where I've the left the carrier bag.

Inside is this dress – red it is, and long, down to the floor – and I can't believe my eyes. I ain't *never* worn a dress like this before! It turns me on, y'know? Just thinkin' that my old man can picture me in a beautiful dress like this, it makes me wet knowing how he sees me. Because buying me this dress, well, it shows he don't think of me as no dowdy wife in my housecoat and slippers like I usually wear. He sees me as the kind of woman who'd wear a dress like this one.

There's more stuff inside the carrier bag. Satin panties that come up round the waist and a matching bra all trimmed in lace. They're red too, but real pretty, not tarty. Well, I put the bra and the panties on, then I slip my feet into a pair of mules, trimmed with red feathers. Those mules have the highest, spindliest heels you ever did see and I feel like I'm gonna fall right off when I stand up.

Then I put the dress over my head and it falls like a silk curtain over my body. Phew-ee – you should see me in that dress! My husband, he wants to pull into a motel, but I say, no way! You promised me a night out, and a night out is what I'm gonna have.'

Eleanor made herself more comfortable on the cushions, intrigued by where this story might lead. She found herself growing to like the interviewee and she could imagine Jennifer stepping out in all her finery, her husband as proud as punch, stealing a few hours away from the children and the cares of their everyday lives.

There was no intrusive commentary breaking into the account and Eleanor found herself approving of Marcus Grant's methods of allowing his subject to speak for herself. This way he allowed Jennifer's personality to leap from the page, and drew the reader in to her story.

Pleasantly surprised by this revelation, Eleanor read on.

'When we draw up in front of this swish restaurant downtown, I can hardly believe it! Loyd and me, we swank into that place, and everyone turns to look at us. I can feel their eyes on me as the head waiting guy shows us to our table. All the men in that room want to be in my man's shoes, and all the women, I can feel their envy. Tonight I am *hot*, you know what I'm saying? [Laughs.]

We eat – oysters that slip down our throats, juicy medallions of beef, still pink in the centre, tiny potatoes all covered in melted butter – and all the time we eat each other with our eyes. I take off one of my shoes and walk my bare toes up the inside of Loyd's leg to his crotch. He's got an erection so hard I swear the material of his trousers is strainin' fit to bust!

"Jennifer," he says, "Jennifer, what you tryin' to do to me, girl?"

But his eyes, they're all dark and smoky and I can tell he's loving every minute. I lean forward to tell him *exactly* what I'm trying to do, but I don't get the chance, because just then, the lights are turned down real low and a spotlight falls in the centre of the room. There's a blast of music, then this gal dressed in feathers and sequins appears in the light and starts to dance.

Well, it's so unexpected, y'know, in a place like that, so fancy an' all. For a minute I just sit there, stunned. I can feel a change in the room, like everyone's getting excited, watching this girl in the middle of the room. And I'm thinking, I can bump and grind as good as that any day!

After a few minutes, I notice that Loyd isn't watchin' the dancer at all – he's watchin' me. And I say to him, I say "What?" and he says, "You can dance better'n that, girl," just like he's read my mind.

Well, I'm feeling so horny by now, I stand up from the table and walk over to the girl. I hear the buzz of excitement that goes around the room, but I don't pay no mind, I'm too busy looking at the girl. She's got her top off already, and her titties are like two little poached eggs, no bigger than that, but sweet.

She smiles at me and waves me over. I start to copy her moves, giving a little shimmy that drives the audience wild.

"Hey, baby – show us what you've got!" they shout.

I laugh and dance harder. I've never felt so alive, so free. It's like nothing matters, like I can't hear nothing, can't feel nothing except the music. The beat is driving through me so that I feel like I'm vibrating. And out there my man is watchin' me and wantin' me . . .'

Eleanor felt uncomfortable. What Jennifer was describing was anathema to her: the mere thought of displaying herself in public in such a way filled her with fear and horror. And yet, vicariously, it seemed that she could feel the other woman's excitement, could identify with her arousal.

But it was too close to the ambivalence she felt about the scene she had witnessed between Michael and Duncan. Disgusted on the one hand, yet unbearably aroused on the other. Such feelings filled her with shame.

Shame, however, did not seem to be in Jennifer's often colourful vocabulary and Eleanor turned her attention back to the text.

'I'm hot; I can feel the sweat running down my sides and between my breasts. It feels like the most natural thing in the world to reach behind me to unzip the dress to my waist. The audience go wild as I ease the straps down over my arms and let the dress drop down to my waist. The rush of cool air against my skin brings me out in goose bumps. My breasts are quivering in the satin cups of my bra and I lean forward to give everyone a better look.

I can't see no faces, but I can feel those eyes on me, lusting after me. God, I feel good! I pull the zip down all the way now and the dress falls in a silky pile round my ankles. The other girl, she reaches out and holds my hand so that I can step out of it. Then she dances round me and unhooks the clips of my bra. My tits are bigger than hers, firm with nipples that stand out proud.

So there I am in my red satin panties and my come-an'-fuck-me shoes, bumpin' and grindin' and struttin' my stuff. And I feel like I'm on fire, like I could take on any man in the room. Hell, I could take on *every* man in the room! [Laughs.]

This girl, though, I soon find out that she's got other ideas. She comes round and stands right in front of me and I find myself staring into her eyes. They're big and blue, like a doll's and there's something in them that makes me feel kinda weak at the knees. Then she puts her arms around me and starts kissin' me.

Well, I ain't *never* been kissed by another gal before. I don't know what to do, so I just stand there and let it happen. It's good – her lips are soft and big and she knows just how to tease my mouth open so that her tongue can get inside. I can feel the tips of her nipples brushing oh-so gently against mine and I feel the shiver runnin' right through to my insides.

Then I feel a tap on my shoulders, and there's my man, come to take over. The girl smiles and steps back, though I know that the way she's looking at me, so disappointed, is the way I'm looking at her too. Except that I'm glad Loyd has come to claim me back.

He picks me up, like I was light as quicksilver, and he carries me off to a room in the back of the restaurant where there's this big, squashy sofa. And then we have the *best* sex we ever had.'

Eleanor put the book aside and lay back on the pillows, staring up at the uneven ceiling. Though she emphatically did not want to do any of the things that Jennifer described, she felt warm and heavy-limbed, aroused in a way that she didn't quite understand.

Jennifer's *joie de vivre* leapt off the page, her enjoyment, her sheer exuberance reaching out and pulling Eleanor in. It was an uncomfortable feeling. If she had had any doubts that the subject matter with which she would be expected to work would not suit her, then reading Jennifer's story had dispelled them.

And yet she was intrigued, fascinated even, by the focus of Marcus Grant's work. What had drawn him into it in the first place? What conclusions had he drawn from his research so far? *Could he help her?*

The rogue thought popped into her head, taking her breath away. Is that really what she wanted – to 'retrain' her own sexual responses? Eleanor lay back on the pillows and closed her eyes. She could feel the slow burn of sexual arousal churning gently through her veins. Surely that was evidence enough that the raw material was there?

It was as if a small light was being shone into the innermost recesses of her mind. Bruised as she was by the ignominious way in which her marriage had ended, she had found it easier to opt for celibacy than to contemplate starting all over again with someone else. Even when Rhys had opened his heart to her yesterday she had refused to even admit the possibility that it might be different with him.

Opening her eyes, Eleanor glanced at the small carriage clock placed discreetly on the dressing table. It was three o'clock already. If she was to be as alert and poised as she wanted to be when she met Marcus Grant, she had better get her skates on; there would be time enough to explore this alien train of thought later.

In the small ensuite bathroom, she sh...
and towelled herself dry, conscious of the i...
of her naked body reflected back at herself in t...
mirror tiles which lined one wall. As the steam
cleared she eyed her neat, naturally slender body,
looking at herself as Jennifer had, assessing. Did
she have the kind of figure that could carry off a
long, red dress like Jennifer's?

Slowly, Eleanor ran her hands down her sides,
tracing the shape of her body. Her skin was warm
and soft, still slightly damp, and her palms slid
easily over the surface. In proportion with the rest
of her, her breasts were neither small nor large,
but firm, the areolae wide and pink, smooth in the
steamy heat of the bathroom.

The indentation of her waist was gradual rather
than dramatic, her stomach softly rounded in a
natural, feminine way that pleased her. Her hips
flared gently from her waist, her bottom high and
reasonably pert, the hair at the apex of her thighs
dark and plentiful. She would have like longer
legs, but had no complaints about the shape of
the ones she had.

Altogether, it was a pleasant enough package, if
unremarkable. Allowing her long, dark hair to fall
over her face, Eleanor pouted at her reflection and
undulated slowly, as if to music. What would it
feel like to have all those eyes watching you
dance? Attempting a sultry expression, she
moved her shoulders the way Jennifer had
described. Her breasts shook, her nipples

35

hardening in response to the sudden movement, and Eleanor put her hands squarely over them, feeling them quiver against her palms.

In the mirror, she saw that she looked like a startled doe and she began to laugh.

'Ooh, you sexy creature, you!' she said aloud, blowing herself a kiss and laughing as she turned away. But although outwardly she laughed at herself, she was aware of a tiny corner of her mind that was excited by the possibility of change.

In the bedroom Eleanor began to dress. With the interview in mind, she had brought with her a smart, light-weight grey suit. The skirt buttoned neatly at the side of her waist, the hem reaching just below the knees. Buttoning a pale blue cotton blouse up to her throat, she pushed her arms into the sleeves of the jacket and stepped into medium-heeled plain black court shoes. With her light, understated make-up and her long hair coiled neatly into a French pleat, Eleanor was satisfied that she looked every inch the no-nonsense businesswoman. Conscious of an inexplicable nervousness, she went downstairs.

They had arranged to meet in the coffee lounge for afternoon tea. Eleanor spotted him immediately, sitting at a small, circular table in the far corner of the room, where, she realised, he would be able to watch the entrance. He rose as soon as he saw her, a small smile playing around his well-shaped lips as he greeted her, holding his hand out over the table.

'Eleanor?'

Eleanor was aware of a tightening in her chest as she looked at him. He really was rather spectacularly good-looking, far more so than he appeared on the television. She had to force herself to meet his eye and grasp his hand in a firm handshake.

Grant smiled at her and she had the curious feeling that his dark, lambent eyes were seeing right into her, divining the thoughts that she would most like to keep private. What did those eyes see when they looked at her? Could he tell how *empty* she had become? Shifting slightly as she sat in her chair, Eleanor tried to gather her fractured thoughts.

'I have to tell you straight away, Mr Grant—'

'Marcus, please,' he interrupted her smoothly.

'—Marcus . . . that I'm not altogether sure that I'm the best person for this job.'

'Really?' He smiled at her. 'Why not?'

Eleanor's mouth opened, then closed again. She had said the first thing that came into her head without considering that he might expect her to explain herself.

'Um, well, I—'

'Only I know how good you are at what you do,' he interrupted her, sitting back in his seat as the waitress brought their tea and scones to the table. 'I read your book on alternative therapies and thought it excellent. You have such a clear writing style.'

'Thank you. If you've read that book you'll appreciate that I like to do a great deal of research before putting pen to paper,' she said.

Marcus raised his shoulders slightly before offering her the plate of scones.

'Of course. The book I propose we write together will need a fair amount of research too.'

Eleanor stared at him as he helped himself to a scone and spread it liberally with butter. Injecting a light-hearted tone into her voice, she said, 'I'm not so sure that I'm keen on that idea!'

Marcus smiled at her, the twinkle in his eye telling her that he had guessed what she was thinking.

'It's not so much of a hands-on approach with my subject,' he assured her. Picking up a buttery half-scone he took a bite.

Eleanor found her eyes drawn to his hands, her gaze lingering on the long, slender fingers. Looking at them, she wasn't so sure that she would want to veto 'hands-on' research after all. To her horror, she felt warm colour suffuse her cheeks. What was the matter with her? She forced her mind back onto the subject of the book.

'May I ask you – why do you want a co-author for this book? As I understand it, you've always worked alone before.'

'I have. However, I feel that I've gone as far as I can, as a man, into the world of feminine sexuality. I've gained a good deal of insight along the way, but with the best will in the world I can't

38

experience the process of sexual awakening from a female point of view.'

Eleanor felt a trickle run along her spine. Dare she suggest that she could act as his guinea pig?

'No,' she said softly, then, holding his eye deliberately she said, 'but I could.'

Several expressions chased across Marcus's face. Shock, surprise and the faint gleam of masculine speculation. Eleanor felt a small thrill that she had been able to provoke such a reaction from him. She wasn't sure how she expected him to react, but she wasn't prepared for his laughter. In spite of her dismay, Eleanor registered that she liked the sound; it was rich and deep and sounded totally genuine.

Catching sight of her expression, he grimaced.

'I'm sorry, Eleanor. You took me by surprise. Look, why don't I give you a copy of the proposal for *Becoming Sexual* so that you can get some idea of what I'm trying to produce? If you could read it this afternoon, perhaps we could then have dinner tonight and discuss it more fully. I take it you are staying in the hotel?'

Eleanor nodded. She needed some time to gather her thoughts. There was nothing in Marcus's direct, brown-eyed gaze that suggested he might be coming on to her and she realised that he had dismissed as absurd her suggestion that she could undertake much of the research in person. Perhaps it was. Of course it was. Then Marcus grinned and his eyes lit up mischievously, making

Eleanor question her own judgement.

'Did you pack an evening dress?' he asked innocently. 'I have a table booked at Two Moons.'

There was no way that Eleanor was going to admit to having nothing suitable to wear to one of the most fashionable restaurants in London, so she summoned up all her reserves of charm and smiled at him.

'Of course. Shall I meet you in the foyer?'

'Make it the lounge bar, then we could have a drink first. Would seven suit you or would that be too early?'

'Seven would be fine.'

'Good.' Now that he had achieved his aim, Marcus was businesslike. 'I'm afraid I'm going to have to rush off – I have another appointment at five. Here,' he reached into a briefcase underneath the table, 'this is the proposal. I'll see you at seven.'

Eleanor returned his smile with every appearance of confidence and watched as he walked away. He had an easy, self-assured stride and heads turned as he past. Seemingly oblivious, he exchanged a few words with the head waiter before disappearing through the doors. To meet a woman, perhaps?

Eleanor frowned as the thought popped into her head. What did it matter who he was meeting? Or, for that matter, whether or not she personally found him attractive? For she did, she realised with a jolt. There was something about the way he looked at her that made her feel warm, but edgy. And she didn't trust him, not at all.

Impatient with the direction her thoughts had taken, Eleanor ordered herself a fresh pot of tea and opened the proposal he had given her. The more she read, the more intriguing she found the subject, especially when she applied it to her own circumstance. According to Marcus, the most unresponsive of women could achieve greater sexual fulfilment by allowing herself to explore her fantasies.

Eleanor raised her eyebrows as she scanned the list of proposed areas for research: massage; pornography; exhibitionism/voyeurism; lesbian experiences; exploring S&M. The final two chapters were to be devoted to the conclusions drawn from the research, discussing, amongst other things, whether the re-enactment of one's fantasies was a valid approach to opening up one's sexual horizons, or whether fantasies should stay safely confined within the mind.

It was an interesting conundrum. Eleanor was intrigued, though reluctantly, by the idea that she might find herself reawakened if she followed the programme Marcus described. If she explored her fantasies . . . Eleanor brought herself up short. What fantasies? Apart from imagining herself with Rhys, which was more wishful thinking than fantasy, she couldn't really say that there were any images she regularly conjured up to arouse herself.

She frowned as a picture came into her mind of herself masturbating to a climax as she had the day before with the image of Michael and Duncan flashing into her head. That wasn't a fantasy, for goodness' sake! she told herself angrily. Signalling for the bill, Eleanor slipped the proposal in her own case. Marcus, it seemed had left instructions for the bill to be added to her account, so she went to grab her bag before heading for the shops.

Later, as she changed into the understated black dress she had found in one of the late-opening department stores Eleanor decided that she looked good. Elegant, but not overtly sexy.

He was waiting for her in the lounge bar. Greeting her with a friendly smile, he ordered her a glass of dry white wine and turned to look at her. He had the kind of eyes that made Eleanor feel that all his attention was on her. She felt his scrutiny of her dress, though she couldn't gauge his reaction from the expression in his eyes.

'What did you think of the proposal?' he asked her after a few minutes.

'I thought it was very . . . interesting,' she replied carefully.

'Interesting enough to work on it with me?'

Eleanor grinned.

'Don't rush me!' she said, feeling a warm glow as he returned her smile.

The Two Moons restaurant was lit by gently

flickering hurricane lamps set into innumerable iron sconces placed around the walls. The table to which they were shown with the minimum of fuss was spread with a pristine white cloth and set with gleaming silver cutlery. Looking around her as the waiter went to fetch a menu, Eleanor saw that all the tables were the same, mostly set for two with the odd larger one set for four. There was a generous distance between them so that there was a sense of privacy, yet the overall atmosphere contrived to be cosy and intimate.

Eleanor chose seafood for her main course while Marcus opted for a steak, cooked rare.

'I like my daily helping of red meat,' he commented, his eyes twinkling in the dim lighting as Eleanor grimaced.

'I prefer chicken and fish. I suppose you'd read something significant into that – something to do with the difference in our sexual drives?'

Marcus raised his eyebrows at her across the table and Eleanor felt her stomach somersault. She had meant the comment to be a light-hearted one, and only now did she realise how it could be interpreted.

'What do you know about my drives, Eleanor, sexual or otherwise?' he asked her, his voice low.

Eleanor strove for insouciance as she shrugged. 'I'm only making the kind of assumptions that you make about women all the time.'

'Oh? And what conclusions have you drawn about me?'

Eleanor considered trying to change the subject, but his eyes challenged her and she was seized by a kind of recklessness that was totally alien to her.

'I would say that, with your professional interest in women and their sexuality, you like your sex frequent and varied. I wouldn't imagine that fidelity is very high on your list, nor even tenderness, for that matter. Your interest is too heavily geared to the mechanical, so the more cerebral side of sexual attraction doesn't appear to interest you at all.'

Marcus stared at her across the table as she paused. His eyes seemed opaque, his expression unreadable and Eleanor wondered if she had offended him. Certainly she had managed to surprise him.

'I'm sorry if you feel I've been too personal,' she said stiffly when he still did not respond.

To her surprise, he suddenly tipped back his head and laughed. From the corner of her eye, Eleanor saw that they were attracting the attention of the other diners and she felt uncomfortable.

'Have I amused you?' she asked icily.

Marcus stopped laughing and smiled at her.

'A little. Have another glass of wine, Eleanor, and then you can ask me all the questions I can see you are dying to ask.'

'You're mistaken if you think I'm the least bit curious about you,' she said.

Marcus smiled again.

'I meant about the book,' he said gently.

Eleanor felt the colour seep into her cheeks. Was this evening really going to be nothing more than a series of blunders on her part?

'Of course you did,' she murmured, casting around frantically in her brain for an intelligent question she could put to him. 'Actually, I wanted to ask you about Jennifer.'

'Jennifer?' He looked perplexed.

'In *Women's Secret Lives*. The woman who went dancing with her husband and ended up joining the floor show.'

'Ah yes. Jennifer. What about her?'

Eleanor felt uncomfortable, half wishing she hadn't opened the subject.

'It's just that . . . I can't understand why she would want to do such a thing.'

'But she didn't.'

'Pardon?'

'She didn't. Eleanor, you're confusing fact with fantasy. Jennifer was describing what goes on inside her head when she masturbates, or when she's making love with her husband.'

Hoping he hadn't noticed her discomfort at his casual references to such intimate acts, Eleanor forced herself to look him in the eye.

'You mean, that scene never happened? It wasn't even something that she'd done once and therefore kept remembering?'

'I don't think so. I don't imagine so. Remember the way she describes herself and the clothes she wears?'

Eleanor nodded.

'Well, the real Jennifer is about five foot two and sixteen stone with a penchant for brightly patterned tent dresses – which suit her very well, I might add.'

'But—'

'Part of Jennifer's fantasy is that she's tall and lithe, the kind of woman who could carry off the clothes she described. That doesn't mean that she's unhappy with what she's got, just that her everyday life is enriched by a little creative fantasy.'

'I see,' Eleanor said.

Their meal had arrived and she picked at it thoughtfully. Marcus's next question took her off-guard.

'What do you fantasise about, Eleanor?'

A brief flash of Duncan and Michael pierced her thoughts and she pushed it away angrily.

'I don't,' she snapped.

Unperturbed, Marcus pressed her.

'Everyone has fantasies, Eleanor – though not everybody recognises them.'

'With all respect, Marcus, that's rubbish.'

The faintest of smiles flickered across his handsome features.

'All right,' he said, leaning forward and steepling his fingers under his chin, 'I'll demonstrate to you. What made you buy that dress?'

Taken by surprise, Eleanor replied with the truth.

'The fact that you told me we were eating here and that I had nothing suitable in my overnight case.'

'Ah!' Marcus chuckled. 'I'm very flattered, but that isn't actually what I meant. Think about what you wanted that dress to say to me when we met tonight.'

Eleanor shrugged.

'That I had the right clothes for the occasion?'

'Too literal. Try again.'

Eleanor shook her head.

'I don't know what you're driving at.'

'Okay, I'll tell you my interpretation, and you tell me if I'm right. You chose black, because it'll take you anywhere and it won't draw attention to you.' He paused, smiling slightly when Eleanor refused to answer. 'The buttons up to the neck say "Hands off – I'm off-limits". So does the tightly coiled hair. That also tells me you want me to think you're in control. What you probably didn't realise when you dressed, was the way the fabric skims your figure as you walk. You've also forgotten the fact that concealment is a powerful aphrodisiac.'

Eleanor stared at him. Indignation warred with a slow, churning arousal that made her push her half eaten meal away, her appetite gone.

'Are you trying to tell me that you desire me, Mr Grant?' she said, angry with the way her voice shook betrayingly. She didn't want him to know that he affected her.

Marcus sat back in his seat and smiled infuriatingly at her.

'What do you think, Eleanor?'

'Me? I think that you are one of the most arrogant, conceited men I have ever met,' she said coolly.

Marcus laughed.

'You see? I knew you were crazy about me!'

'What?'

He waved a hand at her.

'Such careful attention to detail, such contrived signals of unavailability – they could only mean the opposite.'

'Why you – ah!'

Eleanor brought her hand up to shield her eyes as a flashbulb went off right in her face.

'Mrs Dawes – will you comment on Michael Dawes's latest allegations against you?' the reporter said quickly as a bevy of waiters bore down on him. 'Mrs Dawes . . .'

Eleanor waited until the man had been bundled out onto the street before daring to glance at Marcus. He was gazing at her with open curiosity and she smiled a small, bitter smile.

'There you have it, Marcus – the main reason why I couldn't possibly help you with your research. I'd be recognised and that would defeat the object. Your work would be announced in every scandal sheet in Britain and my husband would walk away with everything that we once called ours. I have to go. I'm sorry to have wasted your time.'

Eleanor leapt up and, brushing aside the effusive apologies of the maître d', she rushed straight out of the door and flagged down a cab.

Marcus caught up with her in the street.

'Hey – wait up a minute!' He put his hand on her arm, stopping her from jumping straight into the black cab which had drawn up to the kerb.

'Please, Marcus, I'm embarrassed enough as it is,' Eleanor pleaded, well aware that she was perilously close to tears.

Marcus seemed to be aware of it too, for, peeling off a bank note from a roll that he pulled from his trouser pocket, he tipped the cab driver and turned Eleanor away with unexpected gentleness.

'Let's walk away,' he suggested, nodding in the direction of the Embankment. 'It's okay – he's gone.'

Eleanor smiled faintly and forced herself to stop looking over her shoulder for the photographer who had broken up their evening. Walking alongside Marcus, she was grateful for his silence; it enabled her to get a grip on her feelings, so that she could speak to him without the annoyingly obvious tremor in her voice.

'I'm sorry about that,' she said quietly. 'I was going to explain the position . . .'

'What position is that?'

Eleanor glanced sideways at him and saw that he was watching her intently. Realising that she owed him some explanation, if only for the ruined meal if not for the rest, she wrapped her arms around herself and sighed deeply. It was a beautiful night, warm and balmy. A gentle breeze played across her face, cooling her warm cheeks. The noise of the city created a continuous background hum, yet it was still possible to hear the ebb and flow of the inky waters of the Thames.

'My marriage ended six months ago,' she said, making the words as flat and expressionless as she could in the hope of disguising the hurt she still felt at the events she described. 'These things happen every day, of course. Unfortunately my marriage broke down very publicly. My husband was a Member of Parliament, you see. He had to resign his seat—'

'Because your marriage broke up?' Marcus interrupted.

'No. He had to resign his seat, and I had to resign from our marriage, for the same reason.'

'Can I ask why?'

Eleanor bit her lip, her steps slowing as she tried to find the words to describe what she had seen. 'I found my husband *in flagrante*, as they say, with his secretary. They were on the leather chaise longue which I bought Michael for a "now you've really arrived" present.'

Eleanor could feel Marcus's puzzlement and she was not surprised when he said,

'Sure, that's real sad for you, but why did it ruin your husband's career?'

Eleanor smiled bitterly at him.

'Because his secretary happened to be male. And because I had a friend with me who, as luck would have it, is a freelance photographer.'

'Ah!'

'Ah indeed! Aileen never goes anywhere without a camera strung around her neck. She sold the photographs to a tabloid. Since then Michael and Duncan have been trying to bully me into signing the house over to Michael, hence the smear campaign in the gossip columns. I imagine that was what the photographer was referring to tonight.'

They strolled in silence for a few more minutes, though this time it was a more companionable one. Eleanor sensed a sympathy in the man walking beside her that made her want to reach out and touch him. Restraining herself, she waited for him to speak again.

'It seems to me,' he said after a while, 'that you've had a raw deal lately.'

Eleanor chuckled.

'You could say that,' she admitted.

Marcus smiled at her in the darkness.

'That's the first time I've heard you laugh. You should do it more often – it suits you.'

Eleanor, not knowing how to respond, stayed silent.

'What you need is a change of scene, something to take your mind off your troubles. A new challenge, perhaps.'

'Haven't you been listening to me? Writing is

one thing – that's behind the scenes, fairly anonymous stuff. I would sabotage the whole operation if I helped with the *research* for your book.'

Marcus stopped walking and turned to grin at her.

'Not if we move our base outside London.'

Eleanor stared at him.

'There are journalists everywhere – even in the sticks,' she pointed out calmly.

'People rarely see what they don't expect. To make doubly sure, you could cut your hair—' He laughed as Eleanor's hand immediately flew protectively to her neat French pleat. 'You always keep it hidden anyway,' he said.

Something about the way he said this last made Eleanor's pulse quicken. He was looking at her as if seeing her for the very first time, and when he reached out to touch a tendril of long, dark hair which had escaped from its pleat she shivered.

'How do you bear it, having your hair pulled so tightly back, defying gravity . . .?' His voice was low and seductive and Eleanor found herself leaning against the stone parapet overhanging the river as he reached behind her head and deftly pulled the pins out of her hair, one by one. Each made a tiny tinkling sound as it dropped to the ground, yet Eleanor found she hadn't the energy to protest. As Marcus fluffed her newly liberated hair in a dark cloud around her face, all she could summon was a small 'oh' of distress.

'That's better,' he murmured.

He was standing so close she felt trapped, pinned against the parapet even though no part of him was touching her. His chin-length, wavy black hair fell forward, casting shadows over his face. For a moment Eleanor was sure that he would kiss her and she was aware that she wanted him to, more than anything. The blood was pulsing in her veins, warming her, making her lose her sense of reason. Barely realising what she was doing, she swayed slightly towards him, her lips half parted, her eyelids closing slightly.

'Well, Eleanor? What do you think? Shall we do it?'

His voice, still low and evocative, slowly penetrated the fog of sensuality which had enveloped her. She frowned, not able to make sense of his words.

'Shall we do what?' she asked, her voice thick and unrecognisable even to her own ears.

A shadow of a smile passed across Marcus's face. His gaze moved with deliberate slowness over her face and down to her still parted lips. Without taking his eyes off them, he murmured, 'Shall we write the book together?'

It was as if she had been slapped in the face with a cold flannel. Eleanor flinched, her shoulders straightening, her lips pressing together. The book. What else could he have meant, for God's sake? And she had thought . . . dear Lord, what must he think of her? Summoning a bright smile from somewhere, Eleanor nodded.

'Yes,' she said, 'let's do it.' She saw that her answer had surprised him and she looked him squarely in the eye. 'But I want to do it my way.'

'Your way?' he echoed, clearly at a loss.

Eleanor smiled slightly, guessing that he was not used to being caught lost for words.

'Yes. You are convinced that your theories work, that it's possible for any woman to "become sexual", right?'

'Yes, but—'

'Then I want to be a case study. You can prove your theories through me. You can educate me, if you like. That's the deal. I'll get my agent to contact you when you've had time to think it over.'

Before he could reply, Eleanor began to walk briskly back the way she had come, shaking out her hair so that it swept across her shoulders like a glossy brown curtain. She felt his eyes on her, though he made no attempt to follow and she felt suddenly, inexplicably light-hearted.

Now she had taken the decision to sign the contract Eleanor was looking forward to starting work. More importantly, she was looking forward to exploring the feelings which had been growing within her all day. She had felt something when Marcus touched her just now, something thrilling that she had never thought herself capable of experiencing.

Most of her doubts about the man and his work seemed to have been swept aside by her burgeoning belief that he could help her to . . . what? Find herself, she supposed. And if she could unlock the passionate woman she suspected was trapped within her, Eleanor had a feeling that happiness could be just around the corner.

# Chapter Three

'WYNN-JONES.'

'Rhys? It's me.'

'Eleanor! How are you?' His voice softened as he recognised her voice on the other end of the telephone.

Eleanor smiled; his obvious pleasure at her call both warmed and encouraged her.

'I'm fine, Rhys. I was just phoning to let you know that I'm going away for a few weeks.'

'You decided to take that job then?'

'Yes, I got the contract through today. How are you?'

'I'm fine.'

Eleanor winced at the stiffness that had crept back into his tone.

'Rhys?'

'Yes?'

She paused, the words on the tip of her tongue.

*Don't give up on me yet...* Instead she said, 'Nothing. Perhaps we can meet up when I get back?'

'If you like. You'll call me?'

'Yes. Goodbye, Rhys.'

'Goodbye, Eleanor.'

The line went dead, leaving Eleanor to replace the receiver at her end with a gentle click. *Wait for me, Rhys, just a little bit longer*, she said to herself.

Reaching up, she went to smooth her hair back from her face, frowning as her fingers encountered bare skin. Her new, cropped hairstyle still felt strange and she often found herself, as now, reaching up to brush a non-existent lock of hair off her forehead.

It was time to go. With one last look around the safe, comfortable interior of the small cottage, Eleanor picked up her case and went out to the car. Leaving her key with a neighbour so that she could feed the cats and water her houseplants, Eleanor set off for the large Midlands town where Marcus had already set up his office.

He greeted her on the steps of the elegant Georgian terrace.

'Eleanor!' He took both her hands in his and ran his eyes over her. 'I love the hair.'

Eleanor grimaced, unconvinced. She knew, though, that she looked different. Younger, somehow, and more carefree. Marcus showed her into the small, high-ceilinged study where she was to work for the next six weeks. There was a desk under the picturesque sash window with a word processor plugged in ready for her to start. A small floral sofa was crammed against one wall while against the other a filing cabinet, two shelves and a photocopier vied for space. A telephone-come-fax machine was perched precariously on one shelf.

'Well, will it do?' Marcus asked her.

'I should think so.' Eleanor smiled at him. 'If I could put my case in my room I'd like to freshen up.'

'Of course. Dinner will be ready in half an hour.'

He showed her up the stairs into a comfortably furnished bedroom with a small bathroom attached. Eleanor glanced around at the warm peach and terracotta tones of the room and knew she would be comfortable there.

'I'll see you downstairs when you're ready,' he told her, leaving her alone.

Eleanor pressed the 'play' button on the CD player in the corner of the room, curious to see what had been loaded into it for her. Immediately, the sound of running water filled the room, interspersed by a gentle piano melody which was clearly designed to soothe and relax her. She smiled to herself as she unpacked her case and went into the bathroom. Everything had been provided for her comfort, from an ample supply of fluffy, soft towels to an array of bath oils and cosmetics in the bathroom cabinet.

As she prepared to join Marcus downstairs, she wondered if he had given much thought to the condition she had attached to her working with him. He broached the subject over the first course.

'How serious were you about making yourself a case study for the book?' he asked her as he put down his soup spoon.

Eleanor smiled serenely at him across the polished mahogany table.

'Very,' she replied. 'Did you think I might not be?'

'It crossed my mind that you might be calling my bluff, yes.'

'Why on earth would I want to do that?'

Marcus shrugged, not quite meeting her eye.

'I'm not so sure it's such a good idea,' he admitted after a few minutes.

Eleanor raised an eyebrow at him.

'Oh? Is that because you don't have the courage of your convictions, Mr Grant?'

Marcus looked directly at her and Eleanor saw that the challenge had hit home.

'Of course not. I wonder, though, what you think you've let yourself in for?'

Eleanor placed her spoon carefully in her empty bowl.

'Well, let me see. As I recall, your book proposal sets things down quite clearly. You submit that by exploring every facet of human sexuality a woman can get in touch with her own needs and desires. How are you going to prove that your theory works, Marcus, if not in a controlled experiment?'

Marcus looked uncomfortable, but he was prevented from replying by the appearance of the housekeeper with their main course. He introduced the smart looking middle-aged woman to Eleanor.

'This is Maggie Soames, who'll be looking after us while we're working here,' he said.

'Pleased to meet you, Mrs Soames,' Eleanor said, holding out her hand.

The other woman wiped her hand on the pristine white apron which was tied around her waist and shook Eleanor's hand.

'Call me Maggie, please,' she said with a smile. 'I hope everything is to your liking – do let me know if there's anything I can get you.'

'Thank you, I will.'

Maggie smiled politely and left them to their meal.

'There are other ways of awakening your sexuality, Eleanor,' Marcus said when she had gone.

Eleanor smiled cynically. 'Such as?'

'Perhaps a more personal approach?'

Eleanor laughed. To think she had imagined she would be so in awe of him. He might be a modern-day guru on all matters sexual, but when it came to his own needs and desires he was as transparent as the next man.

60

'Such as sleeping with you, I suppose?' she challenged him.

Marcus held her eye steadily, his expression speculative.

'Would that be such a repulsive alternative?'

'No,' Eleanor replied honestly, recognising that his nearness, and the turn the conversation had taken were affecting her. 'But I like my research to be both thorough and objective. Though putting myself in your undoubtedly experienced hands might well be pleasant, it's hardly scientific.'

Marcus was silent for a while and Eleanor was afraid that he had taken her rejection badly. She was relieved when he spoke.

'Why do you want to do this, Eleanor? A beautiful, sensual woman like yourself – why would you want to put yourself through this kind of experience?'

Eleanor decided that, if she was to enlist his help, she would have to be honest with him.

'Because my husband convinced me that I was frigid and I believe that he was wrong. I need to prove he was wrong, or I can't move on. Please, Marcus – help me.'

Their eyes met and held across the table. Marcus still looked troubled, but Eleanor sensed that he would agree.

'Unless, of course, you're afraid that I'll prove your theories wrong,' she pushed him gently.

'You won't,' he replied bluntly. 'Very well, Eleanor, if you insist that this is what you want.

We'll begin tomorrow on the first chapter – massage. Perhaps you would like to telephone this number now and make an appointment for the masseur to visit?'

Eleanor took the folded newspaper from him. There, ringed in red biro, was an advertisement.

'SENSUAL MASSAGE FOR DISCERNING LADIES BY YOUNG, MUSCULAR MASSEUR. DISCRETION ASSURED.'

The advert was one of several in the personal columns of the newspaper and Eleanor glanced quizzically at Marcus across the table. He was watching her closely and she realised at once that he was expecting her to baulk at the idea of replying to the ad. Though her mouth had grown inexplicably dry and she was having serious second thoughts, she was determined not to fall at the first hurdle.

Marcus handed her a mobile phone and watched as she dialled. The telephone was answered by a woman.

'Hello?'

'Um ... hello. Is that the number of the massage service?'

'Yes – how may I help you?'

'I'd like to book a masseur for tomorrow ... evening.'

'Certainly. May I take your details and ring you back?'

'Ring me back?'

'We have to be sure of our clients, madam – I'm

sure you understand. It won't be more than five minutes.'

Eleanor put down the phone and stared at Marcus.

'Will you stay in the house?' she asked him.

'Of course. It's only a massage, Eleanor. You're the one who's in control.'

Eleanor jumped as the phone rang again. Confirming that she would be free at nine-thirty, she again put the telephone down. Marcus was regarding her across the table, his expression unreadable. She smiled and carried on eating, well aware that he could see through her bravado, but grateful that he kept his own counsel.

At nine the following evening, Eleanor was a nervous wreck. She had soaked in the bath until the water had cooled around her and was waiting in her room dressed in nothing but a thick towelling robe. Sitting at the pretty dressing table in the corner of the room, she stared at her reflection.

In the soft glow of the bedside lamps she had switched on, her skin looked pale and smooth. Her eyes were wide and over bright and her mouth trembled slightly as she stared at it.

'Come on, girl,' she said aloud, 'this is your first step on the Marcus Grant path to discovering your sexuality. You're supposed to be enjoying every minute!'

Earlier, they had discussed how she would plot

her progress in the form of a journal, leaving Marcus to write the more scholarly material for the book. Given the intimate nature of her contribution, her name would not appear on the cover and she was to devise a pseudonym for herself. She had spent the day writing a draft copy of her introductory pages and had found her tension growing steadily as the day wore on. Now, despite the restful music and the leisurely soak in the bath, she felt so tense that she was sure she could snap clean in half.

The doorbell rang, making her jump. Her heart began to pound with a dull insistence and her mouth ran dry. She heard Marcus come out of his study and walk across the tiled floor to open the front door and caught the low murmur of male voices as he showed the masseur up to her room.

'Eleanor?' He opened her door a crack and poked his head round. 'Are you ready?'

'I can't do this,' she blurted, her eyes meeting his in the dressing-table mirror.

Marcus turned and said a few words to the masseur before stepping into the room, closing the door quietly behind him.

'What's the problem?'

Eleanor turned towards him, folding her hands anxiously in her lap.

'Supposing he makes a pass at me?' she said anxiously.

Marcus shrugged. 'I guess you'll either go with it, or politely decline, whichever way it takes you.'

Eleanor stared at him. 'Are you serious?'

Marcus regarded her for a moment, his head on one side.

'It's not too late to call it off, Eleanor, if that's what you want?'

She almost did, but even as she opened her mouth to ask Marcus to tell the masseur to go away, something stopped her. A kind of calm settled over her and she shook her head.

'No, I'm all right now.'

'Are you sure?'

'Yes.'

'Okay. I won't be far away – just call if you need me, all right?'

Eleanor nodded and he turned away. As the masseur walked in she felt her stomach turn a small somersault. He was wearing black trousers and a white cotton singlet with cutaway shoulders which showed off his physique to the best advantage.

He had a body that was worth showing off. Broad, muscular shoulders topped a pleasingly sculpted chest which tapered to a neat waist. His blond hair was cropped and he had piercing blue eyes which crinkled at the corners as he smiled.

'Hi – I'm Oliver,' he said, moving forward to shake her hand.

Eleanor smiled faintly, liking the feeling of his cool palm against hers.

'Yes. Um . . . I've never done this before . . . How does it work?'

Oliver's eyes swept briskly over her as he took a step back. 'Well, if you'd like to lie on the bed?'

He spread a towel over the duvet and Eleanor lay down rather self-consciously on her stomach.

'Er . . . do you think you could take the robe off?' Oliver said. 'I have a towel here to protect your modesty.'

Eleanor's cheeks flamed as she wriggled out of the dressing-gown and lay down again. Oliver laid what felt like a minuscule towel over her tightly clenched buttocks and knelt down beside her.

'Now,' he explained, his tone low and soothing, 'I want you to relax and close your eyes. There's nothing to be worried about. I'm going to massage a medley of aromatherapy oils into your skin. First I'm going to put some music on. Relax.'

Eleanor lay still, wondering how anyone could relax in such a situation. She felt exposed and vulnerable, every muscle tensed ready to leap up and flee if she didn't like what he did to her. So far, she thought grimly to herself, this experience was nothing like the gateway to sensual awakening that Marcus had said it would be.

At the flick of a switch, music floated through the room, curiously tuneless and yet soothing, waves against a shoreline, washing over her senses.

Eleanor gasped at the first touch of Oliver's warm hands at the base of her neck. Slippery with a heavy, lavender-scented oil, they slipped across her skin, smoothing down her back to her waist.

66

'Your husband said you were tense – he wasn't kidding!' Oliver murmured as he began to work on her rigid muscles.

*Her husband!* The idea of Marcus being described in such a way almost made Eleanor laugh out loud. How had she got herself into this? She had to admit, though, Oliver's skilful hands and fingers were beginning to work magic on the tightly bunched muscles in her back. In spite of herself, she could feel her tension gradually unfurling, little tentacles of pleasure working their way through her body. She sighed and allowed herself to sink into the mattress.

'That's better,' Oliver murmured in his low, restful voice. 'Close your eyes.'

Eleanor did as she was told. By denying herself one source of sensory experience, she found the others were magnified. The music seemed to flow over and through her, vibrating in her limbs. She was acutely aware of the sensitivity of Oliver's fingertips as he sought out every tense muscle. Kneading and squeezing until the tension flowed away, he then turned his attention to stroking and smoothing her skin until Eleanor felt she would purr.

When he was satisfied that she had relaxed, Oliver turned his attention to the backs of her legs, working his way down to her feet. Eleanor braced herself for a ticklish sensation as he cupped one foot in his hand and began to work on the sole, but his touch was firm and precise. As he manipulated each pressure point on her foot, she felt as though the effects rippled up her legs and flowed through the rest of her body. By the time he had afforded the other foot the same treatment, Eleanor felt as if she would float away.

'Would you like to roll over now?' Oliver's voice, soft in her ear, made her stir.

'Roll over?' she repeated sleepily. She frowned as she recognised what he meant. 'Well—'

'I have another towel ready.'

She could sense the smile in his voice as he guessed the reason for her reluctance. To some Eleanor knew she might seem prudish, but she simply wasn't used to displaying her naked body to complete strangers and she wasn't comfortable with nudity. Michael's unhidden distaste for her body had reinforced her natural modesty so that it was not until Oliver handed her the second towel and discreetly turned his back while he selected another bottle of oil did she roll over, draping the towels hastily over herself before he turned back.

Oliver smiled at her and gently pulled the towels straight before warming the oil between his palms. He really was rather attractive and Eleanor found her body responding to the appreciative gleam she detected in his eyes as he ran them swiftly from her head to her toes.

Enjoying a back massage with her eyes closed and her head turned away from the masseur was one thing, but having to actually face him as he went to work on her body was rather too intimate for Eleanor's comfort. Whereas before she had finally been able to relax and enjoy the experience, now she could feel herself tensing again, the adrenalin beginning to pump through her veins once more.

Oliver noticed it too and he glanced at her assessingly as he worked on the fronts of her legs.

'Relax,' he repeated lightly. 'This isn't going to hurt!'

Eleanor forced a smile. 'I know . . . I just feel a bit . . . odd, that's all. Don't your other clients feel inhibited about having you in their bedrooms?'

'Is that how you feel, Eleanor? Inhibited?'

'It is a little *intimate*,' she said, hoping she didn't sound as panicky as she felt.

Oliver smiled enigmatically. 'That's what most of my clients enjoy most about my visits,' he said, moving round so that he was kneeling by her head. 'Don't talk any more,' he said. 'I want you to concentrate on nothing but sound and touch. Close your eyes, please.'

Eleanor obeyed him and his hands splayed across her chest, his fingertips playing across the small bones in a way that made her feel as if she would sink into the bed. Her capacity for rational thought slipped away with alarming speed.

His body was too close for comfort; she could feel the long muscles of his thigh pressing against her shoulder. As he leaned over her to massage her shoulders and her chest, she could smell the

69

clean, male scent of him, an intoxicating perfume that, combined with the tuneless beat of the music, made her feel oddly disorientated, as if her head had somehow been disconnected in some way from her body.

Opening her eyes slightly, she watched the play of muscles in his arms and chest as he concentrated on giving her pleasure. The sight of his youthful, well-toned body and the thought of him using it solely for her pleasure made Eleanor feel warm and heavy-limbed. Recognising the feeling as desire, she tried to rouse herself sufficiently to call a halt while she still had her wits about her.

She opened her mouth to speak, but at that moment, Oliver transferred his attention to her stomach. Eleanor sucked in her breath, conscious of the little ripples of pleasure travelling in ever decreasing circles from her hips to her navel. Oliver pressed gently with the heel of his hand and manipulated her soft flesh in a circular movement which made Eleanor want to sigh with delight.

Beneath the towel, which barely covered her breasts, she felt her nipples gather into aching little peaks. The flesh of her breasts felt heavy and swollen. Though she kept her thighs pressed tightly together, she was aware that the sensitive folds of flesh at their apex had unfurled, moistening in response to Oliver's rhythmic caresses.

Through half-closed eyes Eleanor watched Oliver's face. His whole concentration was focused on what he was doing and a part of her mind, the writerly part, filed the realisation away that one of the most powerful aphrodisiacs was to be the sole object of an attractive man's attention.

Eleanor felt as though she were melting into the mattress, her arms and legs weightless, and there was an ache, low down in her womb. It seemed like the most natural thing in the world when his fingertips edged up her ribcage so that they brushed against the lower curve of her breasts.

Her nipples reacted to the innocuous caress by hardening, pressing against the towel. Eleanor murmured restlessly as Oliver removed it, sighing with pleasure as his warm palms covered her breasts.

'You have beautiful breasts,' he told her, his fingers performing their magic over the sensitive flesh.

Eleanor told herself she would stop him, but she was enjoying it too much. Just a few minutes more . . .

Oliver dipped his head and pressed his lips against the tip of one aching nipple. If she didn't stop him now she knew he would open his mouth and draw it in and then she would be lost. She knew then with blinding certainty that she wasn't ready to take things further yet.

'No,' she said quietly, her voice emerging as a croak.

71

Oliver straightened instantly, offering her his hand as she stood up and pushed her arms into the sleeves of her robe.

'I'd like you to go now,' she said shakily, avoiding his eye.

'Of course. Please do ring again it you need me.'

Eleanor glanced at him and saw that he seemed unoffended, perfectly businesslike as he packed away his oils and towels and removed the CD from the player.

'Thank you, I will,' she assured him.

He flashed her a friendly smile as he left and any embarrassment she had begun to feel was swept away, leaving her with nothing but the slow-burning arousal he had invoked with his clever fingers.

Turning towards the full-length mirror which stood by the dressing table, Eleanor allowed the robe to slip off her shoulders. It fell to the floor in a soft heap, unregarded. Her breasts looked full and heavy, the nipples still standing out like two hard little cones. The oil which had been worked into her body made her skin glow in the half-light of the bedroom. She still felt warm, her sex pulsing gently as it remembered the touch of Oliver's fingers on her breasts.

Shivering slightly, Eleanor wrapped her arms around her body and closed her eyes. Her skin felt silky soft, and her fingers moved as if of their own volition down her sides and across the gentle swell of her belly. Leaning her head over to one side, she ran one hand up her neck, caressing the straining tendons before sweeping her hand down again, brushing across the crested tips of her breasts.

It was a featherlight caress, but the effect was electrifying. She began to tremble, her arms and legs shaking as if gripped with fever, a fine film of perspiration pushing through her pores, mixing with the oil.

'Eleanor?'

Her eyes flew open as she heard Marcus's voice, low and resonant from the doorway. She hadn't heard the door open and, turning her head, she opened her mouth to protest at his invasion of her privacy. One look at his face silenced her. He was staring at her, his pupils dilated, his expression swiftly turning from surprise to desire. A slow pulse began to beat steadily between her legs and she turned slowly towards him, her eyelids drooping heavily and her breathing fast and shallow.

'Marcus!'

It emerged as a whisper, the tone redolent of her unspoken, barely acknowledged need and he responded to it at once. He strode purposefully across the room and his larger hand replaced hers at the side of her neck. Eleanor leaned into his palm and sighed.

'Eleanor . . .' he breathed her name, his warm, wine-scented breath brushing her cheek.

Holding herself in readiness, Eleanor silently willed him to relieve the aching desire which gnawed at her belly. There was no time for thought, for reasoning, for the making of choices. There was only the urgent physical need which had to be assuaged at all costs.

Marcus's arm came about her, supporting her as he lowered her slightly, so that her breasts were tipped up to his heated gaze. With his free hand he stroked the swell of her breasts, sweeping the tip of one finger along the cleft between them. Eleanor shivered and sighed, her arms coming up to cling to him as his hand stroked lower, setting her stomach on fire and causing a potent, liquid heat to seep between the folds of her hidden flesh.

The heel of his hand brushed against the soft fleece of hair on her mons and Eleanor moaned softly. Behind her closed eyelids she was aware of nothing but sensation. Her legs parted slightly so that the cooler air of the room touched the petal-soft flesh between them. She sucked in her breath as Marcus's fingers curled gently into the molten heat of her sex.

'Oh-h!' she sighed, her pelvis tipped upward, pressing against his hand.

'Ssh!' he whispered against her hair, his lips brushing the top of her ear, causing little shivers to run down her neck. 'Hush now.'

He began to move his fingers, playing her like a precious musical instrument, anticipating exactly the moment when she wanted the tempo to change. Her clitoris was swollen, straining towards his fingers so that, when he pressed the pad of his finger against it and moved the small bundle of nerve endings beneath the covering of silken flesh, she felt as if an electric shock had passed from his fingertips through to the very heart of her womb.

Her legs felt weak, incapable of supporting her and she leaned more heavily on Marcus as he moved the small bud round and round with ever increasing rhythm. Gradually, Eleanor felt the sensation gathering at the base of her clitoris, building, layer upon layer, until there was no turning back.

And yet, when her climax broke, it still took her by surprise. Wave after wave of the most exquisite pleasure richocheted through her. Eleanor cried out with the shock of it, and her legs buckled beneath her.

Marcus supported her, his fingers pressing against the vibrating bud of her clitoris, drawing out her climax until she was gasping with the pleasure of it.

'Oh – no more . . . no more . . .!' she whimpered, pressing her pelvis against his hand in a way that made a nonsense of her protest.

Vaguely she was aware of being lifted, of Marcus's arms behind her neck and her knees. The bed dipped as he laid her down on it and, for a brief instant, his strong, warm body was covering hers. Then he rose and she shivered at the sudden chill which swept over her.

'Marcus . . .?'

'Ssh,' he said softly.

Eleanor tried to open her eyes, but they felt as if they had been nailed shut. She sighed as the duvet wafted across her naked body, moving her head so that her cheek rested against the cool cotton of the pillow. She heard the quiet click of the bedroom door as he left, but was too weary to realise its significance. Within minutes she was asleep.

# Chapter Four

---

BY TACIT AGREEMENT, they did not discuss the events of the previous evening over breakfast the next morning. Marcus acted as though nothing had happened between them and Eleanor, had she not woken with the pleasant afterglow of orgasm enfolding her, might have thought, from his demeanour, that she had imagined it.

Sitting at the word processor later, Eleanor poured out her thoughts and feelings, searching for catharsis.

At first, there was nothing overtly sexual about Oliver's touch. He was strictly professional, working on each muscle group meticulously until he had induced in me a state of pure relaxation the like of which I have never known before. That feeling of well-being enabled me to shed some of the inhibitions I had about my body and I felt my initial self-consciousness gradually slip away.

It was as if the massage had unlocked my hitherto unacknowledged, deep-seated need for physical contact, something I had denied myself for so long. Stroking is, after all, a basic human need which is fundamental to the development of a woman's sensuality. If nothing else, the massage helped me to become conscious of my own body in a way that I hadn't considered before. The concentrated attention lavished upon it made me yearn for more intimate caresses . . .

And I got them, she concluded silently. If she closed her eyes, she imagined she could still feel the imprint of Marcus's hands manipulating her most intimate flesh. He had only to turn her in his arms and she would have opened herself to him readily, would have welcomed the thrust of him into her body.

Why hadn't he? Eleanor remembered the brief moment when his body had covered hers and she shivered. She was sure that he had wanted to take things further between them. Recalling the tenderness of his gesture as he tucked the duvet around her, she was aware of a yearning, a sense of a need unfulfilled. And for the first time she began to appreciate the very real danger into which she had put herself – that in awakening her sexuality, she could, like a psychiatrist's grateful patient, quite easily become sexually dependent on Marcus himself.

Already her body ached for him and she found herself listening for his footsteps as he moved around the house. Yet when he came into her study at midday, she almost jumped out of her skin.

'I didn't mean to startle you,' he said. 'Lunch is ready in the living room. I thought you might be ready for a break.'

Eleanor smiled.

'Yes. I've almost finished the first section already. How are you doing?'

A shutter seemed to close down over Marcus's eyes, hiding something from her.

'Fine,' he said. 'I'd like to discuss the next chapter with you over lunch.'

'Okay. I'll be with you in a few minutes.'

She waited until he had left before concluding the first part of her journal.


Massage is a pampering device which every woman deserves. Getting in touch with one's own body, learning about its responses, its likes and dislikes, is a useful first step to unlocking the desire within.

After my massage with Oliver, I not only felt relaxed and cared-for, I felt sexually primed. If only Oliver had been a partner rather than a professional, I would have undoubtedly wanted things to progress further.

Perhaps, then, a course in mutual massage would be a good starting point for any couple who wish to improve the intimate side of their relationship.

Eleanor re-read her concluding sentence and frowned. If she was to keep to the point and chart her sexual awakening, the sentence would not be relevant. Deciding she would leave it for now and edit the entire journal when it was completed, she exited from the program and went to join Marcus in the living room.

Maggie had left them a large green salad and a selection of seafood. At the sight of the food, Eleanor felt hungry and she piled up her plate before sitting down in an armchair opposite Marcus.

'I've got a selection of books and magazines here, Eleanor,' he said, indicating the coffee table.

Glancing at them, she saw the lurid titles of some of the magazines and felt her cheeks grow warm. Noticing, Marcus chuckled softly.

'Some of them are pretty hard core – don't expect to relate to all of them. It's important to keep detailed notes of both the content and your response to it. I'm going away for a few days to conduct the interviews I set up before we came, so you have the house to yourself. There are videos too – I'll leave those in your study so that Maggie doesn't come across them when she's dusting.'

Eleanor pushed away her disappointment that

he was going away and smiled faintly at him.

'I . . . suppose I'd better reserve the evenings for the actual reading and watching,' she said.

'It might be wise. You'll be on your own then, so you can have a free run of the house.' He smiled at her, a smile that seemed, to Eleanor, to not quite reach his eyes. 'I'm leaving straight after lunch. You can reach me on the mobile if you need anything. Any questions?'

Eleanor shook her head.

'It seems straightforward enough. You're off interviewing, and I'm going to spend the next few days reading and watching pornography.'

Marcus returned her smile and this time his eyes crinkled at the corners with genuine warmth.

'It's a hard life, isn't it?'

Eleanor waited until she had eaten dinner, making sure that Maggie had gone home before she picked up the first of the magazines. She had seen this type of top-shelf men's magazine before and knew that looking at acres of exposed female flesh was not likely to turn her on.

It struck her, though, as she flicked idly through the glossy pages that, from a purely instructive point of view, this was the only time she was likely to see another woman's vulva in such graphic detail. The differences in something that was fundamentally the same in all women were fascinating. Not only did pubic hair seem to run the whole range of colour, texture and quantity, there seemed to be just as many diverse types of labia. Some were thin, some plump and moist-looking; some protruded below the outer labia whilst others were so neat and symmetrical they hardly looked real. Though none could be described as pretty, there was a certain beauty about those displayed. For the first time, Eleanor began to appreciate the male obsession with female genitalia.

Marcus had included a selection of magazines aimed at women and Eleanor spent an hour gazing at page after page of anonymous, semi-erect penises. Concluding that it wasn't the sight of a male member that was designed to turn her on, but the intention of the man to whom it belonged, she soon cast the magazines aside. She would go back to those later.

There were books, ranging from the vaguely raunchy to the downright obscene. She selected a couple, both purporting to be written by women, for women, in the hope that these might be able to touch a nerve. She had three days, after all, to plough through the pile of magazines and books. Before she went to bed tonight, she would watch one of the dozen or so videotapes.

The one she fed into the VCR was short on dialogue, as if the producer had decided to do without a script and so have his actors say as little as possible. There was a soundtrack which ebbed and flowed according to the drama of what was going on.

The plotline, such as it was, was absurd, but as the protagonists began to strip off their clothes and get down to the real business of the film, Eleanor found herself irresistibly drawn to the images on the screen.

The main female character, a stunning redhead with large, silicone-assisted breasts and long, slender legs, performed a striptease for two men who were sitting on a sofa in what looked like a high-rise office block. The woman stood with her back to the partially closed Venetian blinds and swayed to the pulsing beat of the music which filled the office.

She was wearing a red, figure-hugging top and black lycra mini-skirt over minuscule thong briefs and a push-up bra. Eleanor could sense the tension of the two men watching as she peeled off the last of her clothes and stood, gloriously naked except for her ridiculously high, spike-heeled mules, in front of them.

Apart from the artificially pumped-up breasts, the woman had a stunning figure; firm and slender, the skin smooth and pale. One of the men stood up and walked around her, his eyes raking her body with undisguised lust.

Eleanor felt uncomfortable to be witnessing the scene, but she made herself watch, trying to keep a part of her mind objective so that she could record her responses later.

The men were dressed in smart city suits and their impeccable tailoring provided an erotic counterpoint to the woman's nakedness. The man who had risen stood behind the woman's shoulder, so close that she would have been able to feel his breath against her naked shoulder as he leaned over her.

'Walk for us,' he said, his voice low and silky.

Without a word, the woman turned and obeyed him, walking slowly from one end of the room to the other, her hips rolling provocatively as she teetered on the impossibly high heels. The camera switched briefly to the faces of the two men, recording their anticipation as they watched the woman parading in front of them.

The man on the sofa was stroking himself through the fabric of his trousers. The material tented slightly at the front, and he beckoned the woman over. Bizarrely, the next shot showed her covering her full lips with bright, glossy red lipstick before she sank to her knees in front of the man who stood up in front of her.

As he unfastened his trousers, his cock sprang free, fully erect and eager, brushing against the woman's cheek. The camera focused lovingly on the sight of the woman's mouth, garishly bright, opening to admit the bulbous head of his penis.

Eleanor watched, mesmerised, as the woman's cheeks bulged to admit the man's cock into her mouth. She had never seen anything this explicit before and she was dismayed to realise that a dull heaviness had settled between her thighs, a precursor to arousal.

It wasn't as if she found the scenario being played out before her particularly affecting, it was simply the close proximity of intimacy that provoked a reaction from her. Appalled and fascinated in equal measure, Eleanor watched as the man pushed the woman away. His cock was glistening, rearing up from his groin like a baton.

The other man moved forward now and the woman turned, watching as he took off his clothes. Eleanor found herself empathising with the woman's obvious tension as the man peeled off his tight-fitting boxer shorts. She gasped aloud as she saw his cock. It was huge, bigger than anything she had ever imagined. Pointing upwards, the bulb was level with his navel. Not only was it long, it was thick, so much so that when the woman reached for him, her middle finger and thumb did not meet as she circled it.

Miming her delight at its size, the woman stroked and kissed it while the two men looked on. The camera panned down to her buttocks which the first man began to stroke and caress. Slowly, he parted her bottom cheeks to reveal the shadowed crease between and the heavy purse of her sex below.

The woman's sex glistened as the camera lingered lovingly on the intricate folds of flesh. Eleanor's eyes widened as she watched the man open her with his thumbs, exposing the entrance to her body to the steady eye of the camera.

In one of the swift, senseless changes in

camera-shot which seemed to punctuate the action, the woman was now crouching over the well-endowed man, who was lying on his back on the floor. Reaching between her legs, she opened her labia and positioned herself so that the man's massive cock was poised at her entrance.

Eleanor moaned in unison with the woman as she fed the man's cock into her vagina. The camera showed her sex stretching and bulging around it, before panning to the woman's face. Her expression was a cross between ecstasy and pain, a combination which was strangely erotic.

As soon as she had eased the man inside her, the other man stepped forward so that his feet were positioned on either side of the first man's torso. While the first man pumped his hips in time with the woman, the second man gathered up her generous breasts in his hands, forming a channel for his cock.

Eleanor watched as the trio moved with choreographed precision towards the inevitable climax. The woman's mouth stretched wide, the tendons standing out on her neck and her eyes glazing over as she strained towards orgasm. Her neck and breasts were spattered by the semen pumping from the cock which had been moving between her breasts. Seconds later, her hips bucked as the man beneath her came.

When it was over, Eleanor switched off the television set and made her way upstairs in a daze. After so many months of self-imposed celibacy, the past two days had given her sensory overload. When she had first read Marcus's proposal she had genuinely believed that his programme might work for her. Now she was certain it could, and with a speed that had taken her breath away.

She had never dreamt that looking at pictures and watching other people copulate would arouse her as it had, and she wasn't sure whether she liked the revelation. It made her feel slightly dirty, ashamed of the base nature of her response. After all, the people on the screen had been like two-dimensional images, there purely as objects of sexual gratification. There was something rather cold and clinical about the whole affair that Eleanor found vaguely distasteful.

Nevertheless, there was no getting away from the fact that her entire body felt as if it had been stroked all over by a wire brush – her skin tingled and the blood pumped richly through her veins. Glancing down at her bare arms, she was almost surprised to see that they were as pale as ever – the way she felt, she had almost expected them to glow.

Eleanor paused as she walked into the bedroom, for there on the bed was a small, square box, wrapped in red tissue paper. There was a card attached, written in Marcus's large, confident handwriting.

*Sorry I can't be with you this evening – the gift inside may help.*

Intrigued, Eleanor unwrapped the tissue paper and lifted the lid off the box.

'Oh!'

She had seen dildos before, but never one like this. Made of flesh-toned latex, it warmed in her hand as she picked it up gingerly. It was moulded to look like a circumcised penis, the exposed glans smooth and bulbous, the long, life-like shaft below lovingly crafted with veins and a scrotal sac. Twisting the dial in the base of the balls, Eleanor almost dropped it as it began to vibrate gently in her hand.

As she watched, the stem began to rotate slightly, as if searching for entry, and she turned it off quickly. Did Marcus really think she would use such a thing? It was . . . *obscene*. Masturbation wasn't like scratching an itch!

Shoving the offending object back in its box, Eleanor opened the drawer on the bedside table and pushed it inside. Marcus's gift, however well intended, had taken the edge off her arousal, so she showered quickly and slipped into bed.

It was very quiet in the house and there was barely any traffic noise from the street outside. As she lay awake, staring at the shadows on the ceiling cast by the streetlamp outside, Eleanor was suddenly struck by a feeling of over-whelming loneliness. For a moment her resolve wavered and she wondered what on earth she thought she was doing, so far from home. Then she thought of Rhys, and the relationship they might be able to have in the future, and she banished her doubts.

There were other advantages to this assignment. After the debacle in the restaurant when she had been accosted by a press photographer, Eleanor had not heard any more from Michael and the public interest in her and her reactions seemed to have waned. It was a relief to have the time and space to be out of the limelight.

She was tired. Closing her eyes, she rolled onto her side and allowed herself to drift into sleep.

She was standing on a wide sweep of marble steps leading up to an imposing, multi-storeyed mansion. The sounds of people laughing, the clink of glasses, the dull thud of dance music drifted down to her, as if beckoning her. Her dream-self hesitated, torn between wanting to walk up to the imposing double oak doors which stood open at the top of the steps and wanting to turn away.

As if standing outside herself, Eleanor could see every detail of her own appearance. She was wearing a white dress. It was sleeveless with a neat bodice and a full skirt, cinched at the waist with a narrow, white patent belt. It looked like something out of a Fifties film, very Grace Kelly with the neat white courts and white gloves.

Her hair was pulled back so tightly from her face Eleanor could feel the pressure on the roots. It made her head ache, yet she found the tightness of the bun curiously reassuring, as though it anchored her.

She needed anchoring. Her stomach was churning and she was aware of holding herself so rigidly that her limbs trembled as she walked up the steps. A part of her didn't want to join the party and she didn't know why. It sounded like fun, the merriment growing louder as she drew close.

A large, black woman in a full-length red dress greeted her at the door. The dress was several sizes too small, so that it gaped open across the bust and stomach, revealing rolls of smooth black flesh. Eleanor felt the corners of her mouth lifting in a smile.

'Hello, Jennifer,' she said.

The woman smiled, but didn't say a word. Instead, she pointed along the corridor. Eleanor walked the way she had indicated. It was a long corridor with a slippery parquet floor. There were pillars spaced intermittently along it, giving the appearance of a Greek temple. As she rounded the corner, she heard the unmistakable sounds of love-making coming from one of the shadowed alcoves between the pillars.

Curiosity spurred her on. Drawing closer, she saw that there was a stone bench running the length of the alcove. Over the bench, facing away from her, a naked man was draped over the cold stone. There was another man with him, stroking his naked buttocks languidly, displaying little interest in them as he read the *Financial Times*.

'Michael?' Eleanor said, recognising him.

He looked up at the sound of his name and, seeing it was her, he smiled at her. The other man raised his head, and Eleanor saw that it was Duncan.

'What are you doing in my dream?' she asked, feeling more indignant than upset.

Both men stared back at her with expressions of mild surprise, as if her question had been singularly stupid. Then Michael leaned over and gathered Duncan into his arms from behind. As they turned as one, Eleanor stepped back, stifling a cry of shock with her hand as her eyes focused on Duncan's chest. He had breasts – *her* breasts – the pink areolae visible through Michael's splayed fingers.

Backing away, Eleanor bumped into a hard male body. Turning, she was relieved to find it was Rhys.

'Oh Rhys! I'm so glad you're here!' she breathed. 'I—'

'I can't wait forever,' he said, interrupting her, impatience striping his tone.

'But you won't have to! Just a few more weeks, Rhys . . . Rhys!'

Eleanor clutched at thin air as Rhys turned towards another woman in the crowd that had mysteriously gathered around them. Eyes frantically scanning faces for someone she knew, Eleanor was relieved when Marcus stepped forward. He was dressed all in black, his long hair loose and falling around his face.

'Show us how far you've come, Eleanor,' he said, reaching out to circle her wrist with his fingers.

Eleanor resisted for a moment as he drew her towards him, but it was useless to struggle. It seemed to Eleanor that the crowd moved back, leaving a space around them. She had the impression that dozens of eyes were watching her, feeding on every nuance of her behaviour, intruding on her every thought.

'Those pins again!' Marcus said, shaking his head sadly at her.

For a moment, Eleanor didn't understand what he meant. Then he began to take the pins out of her hair and she remembered how he had loosened it on the banks of the Thames.

'No . . .!' she whispered. She could see by the expression in his eyes that he had heard her, but he did not respond. Instead, he pulled out the last of the pins, sending her hair cascading down over her shoulders.

To Eleanor, the gesture made her feel as vulnerable, as exposed as she would have felt if he had stripped her naked. Symbolically, by letting down her hair, she felt that he had signalled to all those watching that she was a fraud. The neat, calm exterior she liked to project to the world was a sham, hiding the passionate, shameful core of her.

Not any more. Now she could feel the lust in the eyes of those watching affecting her, making her feel wanton and abandoned.

'You see?' Marcus said, his lips against her hair. 'They can all see what you are. There's no hiding any more.'

He began to undo the buttons at the front of her dress, peeling back the sides to reveal her naked, unfettered breasts to an appreciative audience.

'Beautiful,' a male voice said. 'Show us more.'

Eleanor's feet felt as though they had been nailed to the floor as she allowed him to strip her dress away completely. Now she was standing in front of them wearing nothing but the neat, lady-like white gloves, a suspender belt and white stockings, and her shoes.

Her skin blushed under the scrutiny of so many eyes, her nipples rising and cresting as warm breath skimmed them, fingertips, butterfly light, brushing casually across the peaks. Eleanor's breath hurt in her chest and she found it difficult to breathe. A blossoming, moist heaviness settled between her legs, her labia aching as they suffused with blood.

Oliver, the masseur, suddenly materialised beside her.

'Discretion assured,' he said earnestly. 'Open your legs.'

Eleanor obeyed, sliding her feet apart so that he could touch her. His fingers were smooth and professional as they massaged the swollen folds of flesh, working the skin back and forth over her burgeoning clitoris.

'She's very wet,' he told the room at large, 'hot

93

too. It won't take her long to come.'

'No!' Eleanor's cry was anguished, pointless in the face of her escalating fever.

'No!'

Eleanor sat bolt upright in bed, clutching the duvet around her trembling breasts. Disorientated for a moment, she rubbed her hand over her cropped hair, reassuring herself that she could not possibly be that woman standing in the middle of a room, being publically masturbated to a climax.

One thing that was real, though, was the dull, insistent pulse beating between her thighs. Agitated, she pulled the vibrator Marcus had left her out of the bedside drawer.

It felt heavy in her hand, the latex taking the heat from her palm, becoming almost human as she held it. Swallowing hard, Eleanor switched it on and sank back against the pillows. The mock penis slipped easily between the slippery folds of her sex, finding her clitoris with unerring accuracy. As it began to rotate and vibrate, Eleanor closed her eyes and allowed her thoughts free rein.

Images from her dream, of Michael and Duncan and Marcus and Jennifer, mixed with pictures from the video she had watched. Nothing made sense, any more than the dream had done, and she allowed her mind to wander, to travel along paths that bore little relation to reality, where sensation was all.

She saw herself bending over the stone bench,

as Duncan had done. Oliver gathered up her buttocks in his hands and kneaded and squeezed the flesh, indirectly stimulating the sensitive area directly below.

Looking over her shoulder, Eleanor watched as he unfastened his jeans. His cock sprang free, enormous and straight, like the actor's in the film. Incongruously, he winked at her as he positioned himself at the entrance to her body. She gasped as he pushed his way in. His cock filled her, stretching her delicate passage until she could take no more.

The vibrating latex pulsed against the silky, cleated walls of her vagina, burrowing deeper, drawing the pleasure from it, making her clitoris twitch with frustration.

'Yes,' she whispered into the lonely darkness, 'oh yes . . .'

She came then, wave after wave of searing pleasure travelling along her limbs, consuming her, setting her on fire. And she knew that it was not enough, that she wanted . . . no, *needed*, the extra dimension of a man's body, thrusting into her, sharing her pleasure.

# Chapter Five

THE WORD PROCESSOR glared impatiently at Eleanor as she stared out of the window. Conscious of its constant belligerent gaze, she dragged her attention back to her work, re-reading what she had just written.

In conclusion, in my experience it is possible to reach a state of constant readiness, where an awareness of the sexuality inherent in the world around us is uppermost in the mind. By the frequent reading and watching of porno-graphic material the mind can be program-med to respond to the most subtle of stimuli in day-to-day life, stimuli which would previously have gone unnoticed, or otherwise ignored.

After three days and nights submerged in the material Marcus had left for her, Eleanor felt quite out of touch with reality. She had done nothing but read, watch, sleep and eat, and only then when food was put in front of her by Maggie. She had never dreamed that so many variations on a theme could exist.

Before her marriage to Michael, Eleanor's few sexual encounters had, in retrospect, been quite frighteningly mundane. With Michael sex was always a perfunctory event, with him taking her from behind, usually under cover of darkness. She had never dreamt that such a world of sensual pleasures could exist for her as that described in the books she read.

The latex-covered penis had become a well-used friend as she sought to relieve herself time and time again after observing the many varied acts acted and described. Now she was desperate now for Marcus to return so that she could discuss some of her conclusions with him.

She jumped as the telephone rang, the shrill sound breaking into the cloistered atmosphere of her study.

'Hello?' she answered cautiously, half expecting to hear Michael's petulant tones on the other end. Her heart lifted as she recognised Marcus's voice.

'How are you getting on?' he asked her.

Eleanor hoped that he would not be able to tell from her tone just how well she was getting on.

'Fine. I've asked Maggie to cook something nice for us tonight so that we can compare notes.'

'Ah. That would have been swell, Eleanor, but that's what I was ringing you about.'

'You're not coming back tonight after all?' Eleanor battened down her disappointment and tried to concentrate on what he was saying.

'There's something I want to follow up on here in London – I shouldn't be more than a couple of days.'

Eleanor gripped the receiver as the soft sound of feminine laughter sounded in the background and she realised exactly what he meant.

'I see. I'll just carry on then, shall I?' she asked as calmly as she could manage.

'Can you cope?'

'Of course!'

'Did you like the present I left you?'

His voice had dropped an octave, as if he wanted only her to hear what he was saying. Eleanor resolutely ignored the dark thrill that ran through her and answered him with a briskness that she did not feel.

'It was very interesting,' she said.

Marcus chuckled wickedly, making Eleanor's skin prickle with reluctant awareness.

'I've organised a surprise for you this evening.'

'A surprise? What do you mean?'

For some reason, Eleanor felt alarmed. What did he mean, a *surprise*?

'It wouldn't be a surprise if I told you, would it? Get ready as if for going out; all will be revealed at eight-thirty. I'll look forward to reading an account of the evening in manuscript form when I get back!'

'But—!' Eleanor bit her lip as she realised that he had hung up.

The rest of the day passed in a daze of anticipation. At lunchtime, she took herself off for a short walk around the shops to try to take her mind off the evening ahead. Instead, she found herself dwelling on it, buying herself a new perfume and, in a fit of extravagance, an exquisite silk and lace nightdress in a deep ruby red which she promised herself she would wear the first night she slept with Rhys.

Returning to the house, she ate the light tea Maggie had left her, then went to bathe and change. *Dress as if for an evening out*, Marcus had said, whatever that meant. An evening out *where*? With whom?

Trying to cover all eventualities, Eleanor settled for the black dress she had bought in London the day she met Marcus. Her short hairstyle made it look more chic, somehow, and she was pleased with the finished effect as she applied her make-up and stood back to appraise herself in the full-length mirror.

The doorbell rang at eight-thirty precisely. Burning with curiosity, Eleanor went down to answer it. Her jaw dropped as she encountered a man on the doorstep, a huge bouquet of deep pink roses interspersed with gypsophila in one hand.

'Eleanor?' he asked, glancing at the tag on the bouquet.

'Yes?' she replied, her voice faint.

'I am Lars. I am to give you this.'

Eleanor slit open the envelope he gave her and pulled out the plain square of card inside.

*Yours until morning*, she read, recognising Marcus's handwriting at once, *enjoy!*

She gaped at the man who was waiting patiently to be allowed in.

'What the hell is he playing at?' she gasped.

'Excuse me?' The man's forehead creased in bewilderment. 'I am sorry, my English is not so good.'

'Oh. Well, you ... you'd better come in,' Eleanor told him, taking the roses and watching as he strode through to the living room.

Under cover of arranging the flowers in a vase, Eleanor studied the man who, at her suggestion, was pouring them both a drink. He was young, probably in his early twenties, with chin-length, layered blond hair which fell across his face as he leaned forward. Shown to advantage in the suave black dinner suit, his body looked firm and broad, his hands large and capable. They were a workman's hands, square-tipped with flat, neat nails, but too smooth and clean for those of a labourer.

As he passed Eleanor her glass his fingers brushed lightly against hers. They were warm, sending a small thrill along her arm at the brief contact. His eyes smiled at her, the expression in their cool blue depths courteous and appreciative.

'I suppose you're what they call an "escort", are you?' she said as she sipped her drink.

'An escort – yes,' he replied.

Eleanor realised that she found his accent very sexy and she relaxed a little.

'It's good work, is it?' she asked, genuinely interested.

'Yes.'

'What do you like about it?'

The expression in his eyes told her that he was puzzled by her questions, but he smiled as he answered.

'I like to meet such beautiful ladies,' he said.

His voice had a pleasant, sing-song cadence to it that made Eleanor smile. He seemed to be showing a genuine interest in her. Then it struck her that she did not need to worry in the least about the impression she might, or might not, be making on him – his opinion of her was irrelevant. As Marcus had said in his note, Lars was hers for the evening, fully paid for. She could do anything she liked with him. He was hers to enjoy.

The idea grew in appeal as she studied him, less covertly now that she had acknowledged his function.

'You don't mind being treated as a sex object?' she asked him curiously.

His forehead puckered in a frown.

'A . . . sex object . . .?'

'Your English really isn't very good, is it?' Eleanor said, her smile taking the sting out of her words. 'Still, we don't need to talk much, do we? Why don't you take off your jacket, make yourself more comfortable?'

She watched as he shrugged off the jacket and draped it over the back of the armchair. As he moved, the play of his muscles was visible beneath the fabric of his snowy white shirt. What could she do with him?

After her initial shock, the idea of being able to command this young stranger in any way that took her fancy had a definite appeal. Eleanor moistened her lips with the tip of her tongue. Making a decision, she put down her glass and beckoned to him.

'Let's go straight upstairs, Lars,' she said.

Taking her outstretched hand, Lars allowed her to lead him up to her room.

Inside, Eleanor switched on the CD player for a little background music. She had left the bedside lamps on and they cast a warm, womblike glow across the room. Lars stood by the side of the bed and watched her as she took off her earrings and watch and laid them on the dressing table.

The tension in the room was almost palpable, as if an invisible fog of sensuality had enveloped them both, drawing them together. Lars looked quizzically at her, waiting for her to make the next move. Eleanor felt an unaccustomed surge of power run through her veins and she smiled.

Holding his eye, she stepped forward and began to unfasten his tie. She was at eye level with the knot and, as he lifted his chin to make it easier for her, she gave in to the urge to press her lips experimentally against the bulge of his Adam's apple. It moved under her lips as he swallowed and she snaked out her tongue to taste his skin. It was warm and salty and Eleanor felt the adrenalin rushing through her.

She could feel the heat of his potent male body through the thin cotton fabric of his shirt and she wrestled with his buttons, impatience making her clumsy, as she stripped him. His pectorals were like two solid slabs of muscle, the golden skin covering them lightly furred with a blanket of blond chest hair. He shivered involuntarily as she ran her palms over his chest and the flat brown discs of his nipples hardened instantly.

'You have a very attractive body,' she told him.

It was curiously liberating to feel free to make such remarks. Before, she had always been too shy to admit verbally that she had even noticed a man's body, never mind found it appealing. Lars smiled down at her, unthreatening but virile, and Eleanor shivered in anticipation.

'Thank you,' he said. 'Would you like that I undress you?'

Eleanor considered for a moment.

'No,' she said, 'I think I would prefer to have you naked first.'

She could see the query in Lars's eyes, but he

didn't say anything as he unfastened his belt and slowly pulled it through the loops of his trousers. Eleanor watched his face, relishing the tension coupled with a slight apprehension that she could read there. Was this what men felt like when a woman stripped for them? Powerful, in control . . . so many images chased through Eleanor's head as she watched him, replays of the pornographic films and books and magazines which had been her constant diet this week.

Lars was wearing plain grey, jersey boxer shorts. The outline of his semi-erect penis was clearly visible beneath them as he bent to remove his socks. Straightening, he held himself tense as he watched her. Eleanor smiled.

'And the shorts, please.'

His pubic hair was as blond and fine as the hair on the rest of his body. Rising up from it, his cock looked very white, the exposed glans smooth and pink. His balls were full and heavy, the skin pulled tight across the scrotal sac.

He stood very still as Eleanor moved towards him and put her arms around his neck. She could feel the heat and shape of his body through the thin fabric of her dress and relished the sense of control it gave her to be fully clothed while he was as naked as the day he was born.

She turned her head away as he tried to kiss her.

'No – let me explore you.'

'An undiscovered country?'

Eleanor laughed.

'Yes. Do you mind?'

Lars shrugged, but Eleanor sensed that he was excited by the way she had demanded passivity from him.

'I am . . . for you,' he said, his voice low and husky. 'I am happy to bring you pleasure.'

'Good,' Eleanor breathed, 'because you do. Lie down.'

She moved with him to lie on the bed, her body covering his for a moment until she eased herself to one side. Propping her head on one elbow, she ran her fingertips lightly from his throat to his navel. Lars watched her almost indulgently, swallowing hard as the palm of her hand brushed against the swollen shaft of his penis.

Virtually ignoring him as a person, Eleanor explored his body with her hands, marvelling at the essential differences between his body and her own. Where she was soft and pliable, he was hard and unyielding, where her skin was smooth and hairless, his was rough beneath her fingers. Even his feet were different, strong and broad with no suggestion of delicacy.

After a few minutes of touching and feeling, Eleanor bent her head and kissed him. His lips were firm and warm, the inside of his mouth sweet against her tongue. He moaned deep in his throat and Eleanor felt the sound vibrate against her own lips.

'You're hot,' she murmured as she pulled away, her fingers roaming the sweat-slick skin of his chest.

105

'It is the . . . uh . . . *strain*,' he explained with a rueful smile.

'I admire your control,' she told him, smiling, 'but I haven't finished with you yet.'

Lars groaned as she followed the path her fingers had taken earlier with her mouth. Carefully avoiding his cock, which was fully erect now, she explored every satin-coated inch of him, acquainting herself with the taste and texture of his skin.

She could feel the slow burn of arousal growing in her belly and she knew that the time had come to remove her own clothes. Holding Lars's gaze, she stood at the side of the bed and slowly took them off. His eyes darkened from pale blue to periwinkle, growing opaque as Eleanor's body was revealed. The tip of his tongue moved between his closed lips as she raised her arms and turned around slowly, possessed by a streak of mischief that made her want to tease and torment him to breaking point.

'Let me touch you,' he said, his voice gruff and thick with passion.

'Yes – but only as I direct you.'

His eyes registered confusion as she moved towards him.

'My neck,' she said softly, 'I want you to kiss my neck.'

Sitting on the edge of the bed with her back to him, Eleanor closed her eyes in bliss. Lars's lips were gentle as they moved across the sensitive sweep of her neck, planting small, ticklish kisses on the delicate skin. As he moved around to the nape of her neck, Eleanor shivered and bent her head forward. Her breasts were swollen, the nipples gathering into little peaks of desire as he concentrated solely on the area she had specified, patiently working his way across every square centimetre of skin.

How wonderful it was to be able to dictate the pace like this instead of allowing the man to control her! This way Eleanor felt she could ensure she was fully ready for him to move on – or call a halt if she so wished. The freedom to call the shots was liberating, unlocking the deep well of sensuality that, so far, had only been released when she was alone. Eleanor felt her excitement grow.

'Now my back,' she said huskily, determined to make the suspense last for as long as possible.

'You have a beautiful back,' Lars murmured, his warm breath brushing across her shoulderblades, 'so smooth . . .'

His tongue traced the outline of each of her vertebrae while his fingers pressed gently on the tail of her spine, sending a jolt of pleasure through her which resolved itself into an ache.

'My breasts . . .' she whispered, aware as she did so that her entire body had become suffused with heat, her limbs trembling in anticipation of his touch.

Lars seemed to have picked up on her

yearning, for when he reached around her body to caress her breasts, his touch was exactly as she needed it to be; soft and delicate, stroking and coaxing the response from her rather than trying to force the pace.

It can't have been easy for him; she could feel his erection pressing into her back as he moved closer to her, so hard and potent she was sure he was ready to come. To his credit, the only indication of the effort it took him to control himself was in the slight shaking of his hands as he kneaded her breasts, and the quiet shallowness of his breathing.

Eleanor allowed her head to fall back against his shoulder and he immediately pressed his lips against her neck again. His fingers squeezed gently at her nipples, sending spirals of pleasure through her breasts and down to her womb. She could feel the secret folds of flesh between her legs moisten and swell in response to his caresses and she murmured incoherently.

'Let me take over now,' he whispered against her hair. 'I know what it is you are wanting. Trust me.'

Floating on a sea of sensation, Eleanor could only murmur her assent. She *did* trust him; he had allowed her to show, rather than tell, him exactly what she required and not once had he tried to use his male strength to impose his own will on her.

She gasped at the first touch of his fingers

against her mons. The backs of his knuckles brushed against the soft fleece, his fingertips gently tracing the crease between her labia. Eleanor felt her legs part of their own accord and Lars slipped his middle finger into the soft, slippery channels of flesh.

It felt divine, the slow, rhythmic caress of his finger against the uppermost point of her labia, coaxing the small bundle of nerve endings at the apex to slip from its protective hood and quiver against his fingertip. Little trickles of ice water seemed to run through her legs as, with his other hand on her inner thigh, he eased them farther apart, giving him easier access to the trembling flesh within.

Slowly, Lars eased her onto her back and half covered her body with his. His cock pressed against the soft flesh of her belly, but he made no move towards self-gratification as he kept up the rhythmic stroking of her clitoris and its surrounds, apparently enjoying the pleasure it was giving her.

Eleanor reached down and caressed the velvety tip of his glans with her thumb. Lars shuddered, his rhythm faltering for a second as she wiped the thin fluid leaking from the tip around the soft-skinned plum. Curling her fingers around the shaft, Eleanor drew her hand up and down, moving the satiny flesh over the hard core of his cock.

With a muttered oath in his own tongue, Lars covered her hand with his.

'Wait,' he whispered, 'please ... let me pleasure you first.'

He waited for her agreement to show in her eyes, then he dipped his head and dabbed the tip of his tongue against the hard bud of her clitoris.

Eleanor had not expected this, and her hands curled against the sheets as he began to lick and nibble at her burning flesh. Looking down, she could see his golden head moving against the dark fleece of her mons, his tongue pink and coated with the dew of her arousal, moving in and out of her.

The sight tipped her over the edge. Having taught herself to come at will with the dildo Marcus had given her, it was easy to let herself go against his warm, living tongue.

'Oh!' she cried out as her climax broke, meshing her fingers into his hair and holding his face against her convulsing flesh. 'Sweet Heaven . . .!' To her surprise, tears gathered in her eyes and spilled down her cheeks in warm, salty rivulets.

When, at last, it was over, he raised his head and smiled at her. Eleanor could see her own secretions glistening on his chin and she drew his face to hers so that she could kiss it away. Her musk tasted oddly sweet, like thick honey, coating her tongue. Lars kissed her deeply, his tongue exploring her mouth as it had her sex, probing and caressing the insides of her cheeks. With his thumbs he wiped her tears away, gently, making no comment on them. Eleanor was glad she did not have to explain.

'Will you come inside me now?' she whispered as they broke apart.

He smiled and, swinging his feet onto the floor, reached for his trousers. Pulling a condom from the pocket, he unrolled it swiftly over his cock.

'Come,' he said, reaching for her.

Half lifting her off the bed, Lars positioned Eleanor so that she was sitting on his lap, facing him. His thighs were rough against her open sex and she moved her hips slightly, enjoying the rasp of his body hair against her recently sated flesh.

He kissed her again, as if enjoying the anticipation of the moment when he would be inside her. Eleanor looked deep into his eyes and saw the healthy, uncomplicated desire he had for her reflected in their depths. Her sex-flesh stirred again, ready for more indulgence at the thought of him desiring her.

Their eyes held as he lifted her hips and found the entrance to her body with the tip of his cock. Nudging gently, he opened her, then let her sink onto him.

It was like nothing Eleanor had ever experienced before. He came into her so deeply, stretching the walls of her vagina and pressing against the neck of her womb with a pressure which bordered on the uncomfortable, but stopped just short of pain.

111

For several moments, he held her still, as if giving her time to get used to the feeling. Then he began to lift and lower her on the straining rod, the tendons in his neck standing out at the effort the precise movements cost him. Eleanor held onto his shoulders tightly, steadying herself. Her mouth had grown dry and she tried to moisten her lips with her tongue, to no avail. Sweat pushed through her pores, making her skin shiny and slick under his hands.

Lars was breathing heavily and, although he still looked directly at her, Eleanor could tell that he no longer saw her. Locked in a world of sensation, he increased his rhythm, moving his hips now so that he could deepen each thrust.

Eleanor found herself gasping at each inward movement, her fingers clutching convulsively at his shoulders. She was aware of an unfamiliar sensation gathering momentum deep inside her vagina, a kind of mounting tension that demanded release. She found herself grinding her pelvis against his, grunting as his cock knocked against her cervix, sending a vibration through to her womb.

'Oh, God,' she said, her voice no more than a cracked whisper, 'oh . . . yes!'

It was as if a dam had burst inside her, sensation, raw and red hot, ripping through the channel of her sex and coiling like a tension-spring in her womb. She felt the walls of her vagina spasm around Lars's marauding cock, massaging its surface until he too cried out, brought to the brink by her convulsing sex.

She felt him come, felt the hot sperm pulse out of him as they clung together, as one, joined in ecstasy, their bodies stuck together with perspiration. Lars's eyes cleared as he looked at her, and Eleanor realised that he had found the experience just as moving as she.

'It was good, wasn't it?' she found herself asking him.

'Yes – it was good,' he told her, his face splitting into a grin. 'We rest a little and do it again, yes?'

Eleanor laughed.

'Perhaps,' she said, pressing her lips against his forehead in a spontaneous gesture of affection. 'After all – we have all night, don't we?'

'All night,' he confirmed, his eyes smiling at her. 'And I am free for overtime too . . .?'

Eleanor laughed again and they fell back onto the bed, still joined together. Rolling so that she was underneath him, Eleanor stared up into his eyes.

'You knew exactly what to do . . . how I needed you to touch me. How did you do that?'

Lars stroked her temple with the side of his crooked forefinger and stared deeply into her eyes.

'You must know,' he said.

Eleanor frowned, not satisfied with his answer.

'Please, Lars – it's important to me. No one has ever sensed my needs . . . like this, in bed. You

113

don't know me at all, and yet you knew at once how to arouse me. I know I directed you at first, but when you told me to trust you . . . you were absolutely sure . . .'

'It is not so difficult with a woman as sensual as you. Your body . . . it . . . uh . . .' He glanced away from her for a moment, as if searching for the right word. 'It *vibrates*, yes, that is the word. I can feel the vibration of your pleasure and it tells me how to make it more.'

He bent to kiss her before withdrawing slowly from her. Eleanor watched him through half-closed eyes as he padded to the bathroom and back again, unselfconscious in his nakedness, perfectly at ease with her.

She thought about what he had said and gradually allowed herself to believe him. She had never thought of herself as a sensual woman before. Inhibited, unresponsive, cold, even, but never the opposite of these. Yet Lars had no reason to lie to her, nor even flatter her unduly. He could have walked in, made love with her, and left, the entire transaction over within the hour. Yet here he was, climbing into bed beside her, his beautiful, virile body already stirring in anticipation of the hours to come.

Eleanor saw herself through his eyes and felt her own body respond to his perception of her. Because he knew nothing whatsoever about her, he had no preconceptions about what she would be like in bed, just as she had none about him.

They had come together purely for sex; neither expected any more from the other than this one night.

It was a liberating concept. Lars thought she was a sexy, sensual woman, so that was what she was. Moving into his waiting embrace, Eleanor revelled in this newly discovered facet of her personality and prepared to explore it to the full.

# Chapter Six

BY THE TIME Lars had left the next morning, Eleanor was exhausted, both physically and emotionally. They had made love four times more during the night and for the first time in her life, Eleanor had experienced the type of multiple orgasms she had only ever read about before. Time after time under the diligent attention of Lars's fingers, lips and tongue, her clitoris had throbbed, her vagina convulsing around the sure thrust of his cock as he came into her, setting off ripples of sensation that seemed to consume her from head to toe.

Once inhibition had been thrown to the wind, Eleanor found herself sinking ever further into a physical plane where nothing mattered but the pursuit of sensual pleasure. Lars was an enthusiastic partner, joining her in a tireless quest for pleasure that took them through the long, cloistered night.

As her confidence increased, he was acquiescent as she explored his body once more with her lips and tongue, running the tip along the tumescent shaft of his penis and enclosing the bulbous tip between her lips. She loved the way he moaned as she took the length of him into her mouth, loved the taste and texture of his cock as she sucked and licked and kissed the velvety skin.

By dawn she was exhausted, her body stiff and sore, but pleasurably so. Finally, as the birds serenaded them enthusiastically from a branch outside her window, they slept, coiled together contentedly beneath the duvet.

As he kissed her goodbye at the door, Lars looked as drained as Eleanor felt.

'I will see you again, yes?' he said, his voice still smoky with spent passion.

Eleanor knew that was unlikely, but she kept her own counsel. He had been so good to her, so willing to let her bend and shape him to her every whim, and despite the fact that his time had been bought by Marcus, she didn't want him to go away feeling used.

'Perhaps,' she told him, running her fingertips down the side of his face.

Lars caught her hand in his and pressed a small kiss into the centre of her palm. Eleanor shivered, her body stirring with remembered pleasure.

'Thank you,' she said.

'Thank you?' he repeated, his forehead screwing up in puzzlement.

'Never mind,' Eleanor told him, leaning forward for one last, lingering kiss.

Alone again, she went back to bed. The sheets smelled of Lars; of fresh sweat and sex, and she snuggled into them, feeling warm and satisfied. He had been so gentle, so sensitive to her needs and she knew that, no matter how their night together had come about, she would always be grateful to him.

And to Marcus. If he hadn't hired Lars for her pleasure, she would never have taken such a giant step forward in her 'education'. Sighing contentedly, Eleanor closed her eyes and allowed herself to drift into a heavy sleep.

In her dreams, she found herself dancing with Rhys. His strong arms held her loosely, but close enough for her to feel the heat of him. She sensed that her nearness was as arousing to him as his was to her and she felt happy, light-hearted in a way she had not felt for a long time.

After a few moments, she leaned towards him and whispered in his ear.

'Let's go back to the hotel,' she said, her voice reverberating with desire.

Rhys's arms tightened reflexively around her and she felt the sudden tension invade his limbs.

'Yes,' he said, 'we could—'

Eleanor sat up with a start, wrenched from the

pleasant little dream by the discordant shrill of the telephone. Fumbling for it, she pressed the receiver against her ear.

'Hello?'

'Eleanor? Is that you? You sound half asleep!'

For a moment as she registered Rhys's voice, Eleanor felt disorientated, unsure whether she was awake, or still dreaming.

'Rhys?'

'Yes. Are you all right? You sound a little odd, *cariad*.'

Eleanor smiled, the note of concern in his voice warming her.

'I'm fine, Rhys. It's lovely to hear from you – I . . . I was just thinking about you.'

'Were you?' He sounded pleased. 'We must be in tune, then, if we think of each other at the same time. I was phoning to tell you that I have to go to a meeting in Birmingham tomorrow. I'm staying overnight and I wondered if you could meet me for dinner? If you can get away from your project, of course,' he added hastily, as if afraid that she might make some excuse not to see him.

'For you, of course I can!' she assured him. 'Just let me grab a pen and I'll jot down the details.'

After she had put the phone down, Eleanor felt light-hearted. The thought of seeing Rhys now, when she had discovered that she might, after all, have something to offer him, was so exciting and she looked forward to it with a passion. Would he notice the difference in her? And, if he did, would that encourage him to wait?

Hugging her hopes to her, Eleanor sank back onto the pillows with a sigh.

He was waiting for her in the foyer of the hotel. For a moment, as she lingered in the doorway, she was able to observe him before he saw her. Eleanor's heart turned over in her chest as she saw how handsome he looked, as at home in the dark grey business suit he was wearing as in the rugby shirts and trackpants he favoured off-duty.

His handsome face lit up in a smile as he saw her and she walked quickly towards him, eager to feel the warmth of his skin against hers as he took both her hands in his.

'Rhys! It's lovely to see you!' she said at once.

He was looking at her intently, his perceptive, light-blue eyes scanning her features minutely.

'What is it?' she said after a moment, unnerved by his scrutiny. 'What's wrong?'

He smiled and shook his head.

'I'm sorry – you look . . . different somehow. Happier, certainly.'

Realising at once that he was probably thinking there might be some other cause to her happiness than seeing him, Eleanor sought to reassure him.

'It's done me good to get away, Rhys. I don't think I'd realised quite how badly Michael's harassment was bringing me down.'

He touched her hand in a small gesture of sympathy.

'That reminds me – I have a message for you from Amy on that front. She'll be writing to you, of course, but she thought you might like to know in the meantime. She's issued the injunction you talked about before you left and is currently talking to Michael's lawyer with a view to reaching an amicable settlement.'

'Thank goodness! You don't know how much that takes off my mind,' she told him.

She was glad now that she had given into pressure to get nasty with Michael – it seemed that at the first sign of her being willing to fight back with a lawyer of her own, he had rolled over and admitted defeat.

'Please thank Amy for me.'

'You can thank her yourself, when you come home.'

There was a question in his eyes as he said this, a question that Eleanor was not ready to answer just yet. Ignoring it entirely, she smiled at him.

'Duncan will be furious!' she said mischievously.

To her relief, Rhys laughed and the mood between them lightened.

'Good. Let's not talk about that any more. Tell me about your work.'

Eleanor sipped the dry martini he ordered for her in the hotel bar and regarded him steadily. She didn't want there to be any secrets between them, but she knew he would never understand the path she had taken with her research. He must never find out that she was the pseudonymous woman who was writing a journal in a book called *Becoming Sexual*!

'It's going well,' she said cautiously, 'and I'm enjoying it, but that's mainly because I've also been embarking on what you might call a journey of self-discovery.'

'Oh? Explain, *cariad* – I'm not sure I understand.'

Seeing the wariness in his face, Eleanor leaned forward and kissed him gently on the lips.

'It's nothing to worry about, darling,' she said softly. 'It can only benefit us.'

Clearly taken aback by her sudden, uncharacteristic display of affection, Rhys traced the outline of her lips with his forefinger.

'Is there an "us", Eleanor?' he asked softly.

'I hope so. You've been so patient, I couldn't have asked for more understanding from you. Just another three weeks, Rhys – can you give me that long?'

'As long as it takes,' he replied, his voice catching with emotion. Then he grinned. 'Do you think we could eat in the meantime? – I'm famished!'

Laughing, Eleanor took his arm and they walked out of the bar together, in perfect accord.

' "With the pressure of having to compete, to *perform* removed, I felt free to explore my own desires. A man paid to do one's bidding has sold his right to expectations of his own, and although Lars was undoubtedly satisfied with his assignment for his own sake, his enjoyment was no more than a side issue, a by-product of my own." '

Marcus stopped reading aloud from her journal and regarded Eleanor from across the room. His eyes sparkled at her knowingly, his lips curving into a smile.

'So, Eleanor,' he said, leaning back in his seat and stretching his long legs out in front of him, 'what do you think of the programme so far?'

Eleanor picked up her wine glass and sipped at the champagne he had brought back with him.

'You want me to admit that I was wrong, don't you?' she said, half smiling at him. Marcus feigned shock.

'Would I be so petty?'

'Absolutely! I'll reserve judgement, anyway, until the end of the book. You'll know how I feel when you read the last chapter.'

'Fair enough. Going back to Lars – your account is fairly comprehensive, but you don't explore why you think you responded to him so readily.'

Eleanor smiled faintly.

'I think you already know the answer to that question, Marcus.'

'I do? Refresh my memory.'

'You'd primed me. First with the massage and . . . what came after . . .' It was the first time either of them had referred, even obliquely, to Marcus's appearance in her room that evening and Eleanor hurried on, dropping her eyes from his. 'Then this past week, having me closet myself away with tapes and books and magazines with only a vibrator for company.'

Marcus frowned and shook his head.

'Are you saying that it was merely that you were desperate? That any man would do?'

Eleanor considered for a moment.

'In a way, yes, any man would have served the purpose.' She blushed as she said this, aware of how cold it sounded. 'I was fortunate in that Lars was a very attractive young man. Maybe if he hadn't appealed to me, I would have sent him away again. Who knows? The liberating thing was realising that I wasn't under any obligation to sleep with him whatsoever.'

Marcus was silent for a moment and Eleanor could see that his inquisitive therapist's mind was dissecting what she had said.

'Is that how you feel about sex?' he asked her eventually. '*Obliged* to take part?'

Eleanor grimaced, aware of how that sounded.

'In a way, yes. So many men contrive to make you feel like that. They take you out and buy a meal . . . maybe they don't always realise it, but there's *pressure* applied, very often, every step of the way. They've only just met you, and they expect a response.'

'Don't you ever feel like sleeping with a man you've only just met?'

'But that's what I was trying to explain in that chapter – when the pressure was removed, yes, I *did* want to sleep with Lars. Without that sense of obligation, I felt free to follow my own inclination. Now I simply have to transfer that sense of freedom to my everyday life – escorts are all very well, but they are an expensive form of self-gratification!'

Marcus smiled slightly.

'I hope it *will* be simple, Eleanor,' was all he said.

'It won't be, but at least now I know that I have the capacity for spontaneous sexual arousal.'

'Yes. Time to move on, I think, to the next stage.'

'Which is?'

Marcus smiled at her enigmatically.

'You'll see tomorrow night.'

Eleanor paused at the entrance to the club and Marcus glanced quizzically at her.

'Okay?' he asked her.

She hesitated for only a moment more before nodding and preceding him inside. She should have guessed when he presented her with this outfit to wear that this would be no ordinary club. Dressed in a black, rubberised shorts suit which, though surprisingly light to wear, moulded her every curve, she would have looked out of place in an ordinary nightclub.

Eleanor saw herself now as they descended a

staircase which was made entirely of mirrors. She looked good in the outlandish outfit, her legs long and sleek in opaque black tights, shown to their best advantage in a pair of high-heeled sandals. The suit zipped up at the front and the elaborate silver ring-pull at her throat served as her only jewellery.

She barely recognised herself hiding behind the sophisticated make-up she had felt went with the outfit. Full, moist-looking lips were emphasised in deep red lipstick while her eyes, heavily ringed with kohl and mascara, appeared overly bright, lit from within by a potent mixture of apprehension and excitement.

At the bottom of the stairs, their tickets were checked again before they were shown into a dark, windowless room, filled with some twenty or so single pedestal, glass-topped tables which were arranged around a small, circular stage. No one paid much attention to their arrival, but as they made their way through the tables to the one allocated to them, Eleanor was aware of several pairs of eyes appraising her.

For the first time in her life such attention did not embarrass her. She knew she looked good and she was proud of the visual impact her looks clearly had on those around her. Lifting her chin, she swept the room with a bold glance, a small smile playing around her lips.

'Champagne?' Marcus asked her as she took the seat to his left, facing the stage.

'That would be lovely,' she replied, holding his eye and smiling at him as he gazed at her.

'You're looking perfectly edible tonight,' he told her after a few minutes.

Eleanor smiled.

'I know,' she said with a wicked smile. 'Did you see the other men looking at me?'

'Not just the men,' Marcus said.

Eleanor's smile turned to a frown.

'Don't be ridiculous!' she snapped, uncomfortable with the way his eyes were scrutinising her, missing nothing.

There was a small band situated on a podium at the opposite end of the room to the stage, playing jazz. A thick pall of smoke hung in a dense cloud just above the occupants' heads. Eleanor's eyes smarted at the tobacco fumes, her nose detecting the sweeter, fainter scent of marijuana in the air.

Glancing around the room, she saw that most of the clientele were in pairs, various combinations of men and women. All were fully engrossed with their partners, glancing up only every now and again to assess a newcomer, as they had her, or to signal to a waiter that glasses needed replenishing. There was a curiously intent atmosphere in the room, a sense of expectancy that had Eleanor intrigued.

'What *is* this place?' she asked Marcus.

He watched her for a moment, as if deciding how much to tell her.

'It's a branch of a very exclusive, international

club,' he said at last.

'A club? Are you a member?'

'An honorary one, on account of my research. I wouldn't want to pay to belong.'

'Oh? Why?'

Marcus glanced around them.

'An evening here, or at any of the other venues, can be very diverting, but it is possible to over-salt the egg!'

'What do you mean?'

He shrugged.

'Same faces, same champagne, same entertainment.' He grinned suddenly. 'Don't take any notice of me – you'll enjoy the show. If I sound jaded, it's because I am. Don't allow my mood to affect yours.'

'I won't,' Eleanor assured him, her attention distracted by the arrival of a stunning-looking woman, dressed from head to toe in scarlet feathers. Marcus turned his head to follow her gaze and, to Eleanor's surprise, his face split into a smile.

'Jeanette!'

He rose, his arms opening wide as the exotic-looking creature rushed up to them, her red-stained lips stretching across her teeth in a surprised grin.

'Marcus! Baby – what are you doing here?'

'Another book. And you?'

The woman shrugged and grimaced.

'Just hanging around. You know me!'

Eleanor watched the exchange with a definite sense of having been forgotten. She had never seen Marcus display such open warmth and affection and she was ashamed to realise that watching him lavish it on another woman gave her a pang that could only be identified as jealousy. The couple made no move to draw apart, staring deeply into each other's eyes as they spoke in soft tones, words which she couldn't quite catch. Then the woman glanced in her direction, and Eleanor realised that they were talking about her.

Just as she was beginning to resent Marcus's casual attitude towards her, she was suddenly drawn into the conversation.

'Eleanor, this is Jeanette, an erstwhile colleague of mine.'

Jeanette made a face at that and leaned across the table to offer Eleanor a languid hand.

'Don't listen to a word he says – I never do!'

She smiled at Eleanor with a genuine warmth and Eleanor found herself drawn to her in spite of herself.

'Won't you join us for the show?' Marcus said, signalling for the waiter to bring another chair.

Jeanette's eyes met Eleanor's across the table and she smiled.

'I should be meeting someone . . . but until they arrive, it'll be a pleasure!'

No sooner had she sat down than the mood of the music being played seemed to changed, slowing and altering in such a way that a new alertness travelled around the room. People shuffled in their seats, their eyes never far from the small stage which was now lit softly.

Eleanor had heard of live sex shows, and guessed that this was what was about to take place. She felt apprehensive, never having seen a man and a woman making love in the flesh before, yet she was also aware of a growing excitement. Perhaps it was the atmosphere of the room, catching her up in the sense of expectation, making her part of the proceedings.

After a few minutes, a man appeared and began to dance. He was young, in his early twenties, with a well-honed body and sleek, shiny brown skin. Wearing loose trousers and a singlet, he danced as if his heart would break, his body at one with the music which filled the room.

Soon he was joined by another dancer. This one was slightly built, but wiry and he kept pace with the first man, mirroring his movements as closely as if he was a shadow.

Eleanor was struck by the beauty of the two men. The first was blond, with a strong, square-jawed profile and a powerful physique. The second was dark, with an almost ethereal quality to his face that put him beyond mere attractiveness. As she watched them dance, Eleanor found herself growing more and more uneasy. There was something about the way they were moving together that made her feel

130

uncomfortable, though she could not have put her finger on the cause.

'What do you think?' Marcus whispered.

Eleanor glanced at him, frowning as she saw the expression in his eyes. He looked . . . excited – that was the only word she could think of.

'They're very good,' she replied politely.

Jeanette smiled at her and leaned across the table.

'Luke is my brother,' she said, pointing at the dark-haired man.

Eleanor nodded and turned her attention back to the stage. The two men were sweating profusely now, both from their efforts and from the heat of the stage-lights which illuminated them. They circled each other like combatants, reminding Eleanor of ancient gladiators in a ring, yet still her unease remained. Suddenly, the first man reached forward and, putting his hand at the back of the other man's neck, pulled him forward, crushing his mouth against his and kissing him deeply.

At once, the image of Michael pounding into Duncan's body in his office came back to fill Eleanor's mind. As always, anguish was tempered by a swift, shameful flare of arousal and Eleanor made a small sound of distress in the back of her throat, attracting Marcus's attention.

'Why have you brought me here?' she hissed furiously, her hands curling into fists in her lap.

Marcus regarded her steadily.

'To face your fear,' he said simply.

131

'What's that supposed to mean? Get me out of here!'

Marcus put his hand on her arm before she could stand up. On the stage, the two men were slowly undressing each other, and a couch had been wheeled centre-stage.

'Sit still. Watch – think of it as research. Remember you're supposed to be recording your responses.'

'I only have one response, as well you know – disgust!'

'Don't lie to yourself, Eleanor. Allow whatever feelings occur to come through. Sodomy is no more than another aspect of sexuality.'

Eleanor was about to respond, when she heard Jeanette say, 'Oh, isn't he beautiful!'

Her eyes switching automatically back to the stage, Eleanor saw that Jeanette's brother was dancing now dressed only in his jersey boxer shorts. They clung lovingly to the outline of his cock which was already erect, forming a proud ridge against the fabric.

'I can't watch this,' she murmured, half to herself.

'You can. You must. Trust me on this, Eleanor – I haven't been wrong so far, have I?'

Eleanor pulled her hand away from his and folded it tightly with the other one in her lap. She didn't want to watch this, didn't want to reawaken the way she had felt on that dreadful day when her marriage had finally died. She *wouldn't* watch, no matter what Marcus said. He was wrong to have forced this on her without warning. She would wait until it was over, and then she would get up and leave, if necessary on her own.

The music changed its mood once more, dropping the volume, making the audience feel more involved in what was taking place before them. Reluctantly at first, Eleanor raised her eyes to the stage.

Her heart began to beat a little faster, and her mouth ran dry. The blond man was rubbing a heavy, sweet-smelling oil between the darker man's buttocks as he lay over the arm of the couch. From where she was sitting, Eleanor could not see the prone man's face; he was completely de-personalised to her.

To her horror, she realised that her sex-flesh had moistened in sympathy with him, that she too quivered in anticipation as the blond man positioned his condom-encased penis. All her nerve-endings jumped as he sank into the willing young body beneath him.

'Oh God!' she whispered, her fingers flying to her lips as she was unable to drag her eyes away from the scene.

Marcus put his arm around her shoulders and drew her close. Though she was still angry with him, Eleanor welcomed the support he offered her and leaned into him. She didn't think she was capable of sitting upright on her own, for her body trembled with suppressed emotion, a pulse beating steadily between her thighs, sending little shock waves through her system.

The tempo of the music began to climb, spiralling to a crescendo in perfect accord with the activity on the stage. As the participants writhed in the throes of ecstasy, Eleanor closed her eyes and allowed Marcus to take her full weight.

She didn't quite know how she got out of that room. Afterwards she had a vague memory of saying goodbye to Jeanette, and of Marcus leading her out into the cool night air, but she did everything in a daze, past and present jostling in her head until they seemed to merge and become one. In the taxi Marcus summoned, she leaned forward and put her head in her hands, trying to contain the memory of shock and anguish.

Marcus didn't try to talk to her until they were inside the house. Shepherding her into the living room, he poured her a stiff drink and sat close to her on the sofa.

'Why did you put me through that?' she asked after a few minutes.

'How do you feel?'

Eleanor felt anger surge along her veins and she glared at him.

'Stop bloody analysing me! My feelings aren't just an interesting phenomenon for you to dissect and disseminate all the time! I'm a human being, Marcus, and human beings have a habit of not fitting neatly into proscribed behaviour modules.'

Marcus made no response to her tirade, but merely watched her intently, making her feel like an insect on a pin under his microscope. Finally, Eleanor could stand it no longer.

'Answer me, damn you!' she said, leaning forward aggressively.

Marcus put his drink aside and held her eyes. 'Why are you so angry?'

His tone was so reasonable, so professionally soothing, that Eleanor felt her temper snap.

'Because you used me, you bastard!' she shouted, accompanying her words with a light blow to his upper arm.

Marcus caught her arm as she would have struck him again and pulled her bodily against him. Eleanor fought against the constriction, outraged that he was holding her in what, in any other circumstances, would have been an embrace.

'Let go of me!'

'Calm down, Eleanor—'

'Don't tell me to calm down! You knew what happened tonight would upset me! You knew and you still let me go through it. I don't understand you!'

'Be still and I'll explain.' He waited until she stopped struggling, though he made no move to release her. 'You asked me once about fact and fantasy. Seeing your husband with another man was fact – cold, hard fact. Your physical response to that memory has more to do with fantasy – you

135

never wanted to see Michael making love to a man, but the idea of it, whether you were aware of it or not, turned you on.'

'No.'

'Yes. Only now your fantasy is spoiled by feelings of shame and emotional anguish. I thought that seeing two other men acting out a fantasy scenario might help you to divorce the one thing from the other.'

'Of all the stupid, arrogant, wrong-headed—'

Her angry words were smothered by Marcus's mouth descending on hers. There was no gentleness in the kiss, only a desire to silence her, and Eleanor fought against it, gritting her teeth against the onslaught of his tongue and holding her body rigid in his arms.

Gradually, the kiss changed, became more yearning and less angry, and Eleanor began to relax into his embrace. A part of her was determined to hang onto her anger, to fight him, but the greater part of her wanted the slow burning desire triggered by the scene she had witnessed to be assuaged.

Pressing herself against him, she felt the heavy thud of his heart, felt the warmth of his skin through his clothes and her own body began to clamour for release.

'Marcus,' she murmured, her lips moving against his mouth, 'please . . .'

She wasn't sure what she was pleading for, she only knew that she wanted him, suddenly, with a ferocity which took them both by surprise. He did not resist her as she fumbled for the belt of his trousers and pulled the end through the guide. She could feel his erection growing in response to her sudden, unexpected assault and she worked feverishly at the fastening to his trousers.

Meanwhile, Marcus's hands were everywhere; at her waist, her breasts, the curve of her bottom as he searched for a way into the tight-fitting rubber suit. Eleanor freed his penis, then reached down between her legs to unsnap the press-studs at her crotch.

She was naked underneath it. The heat of her sex was shocking as she caressed herself briefly. Taking Marcus's hand, she covered his fingers with her own and pressed them into the hot, wet well of her sex.

'Fuck me, Marcus,' she murmured in a voice she didn't recognise as her own.

'Eleanor—'

'Now, Marcus – come inside me.'

She was desperate, not daring to think that he might refuse her. She couldn't bear it if he did, if he should reject her now when she needed nothing more than a hot, hard cock thrusting into the softness of her body. Lying back on the sofa, she opened her legs slowly, displaying herself to him as he gazed at her.

Beads of sweat stood out on his forehead and upper lip and his cock reared up from his open fly, indisputable evidence that he was as aroused as she. He seemed to come to a decision. Holding her down by the shoulders, he covered her body with his and, without preamble, thrust into her with one sure, firm stroke.

Eleanor squealed as he pumped his hips back and forth, each time making his penetration deeper, harder, closer to what she really needed for him. His hands on her shoulders were not gentle, yet somehow the sensation of being held down added to the desperate need that was clawing at her insides, compelling her to meet him thrust for thrust.

Holding his gaze, she was aware that it was a battle of wills, that he no more wanted to be the first to come than she did. Then suddenly she was past caring and she welcomed the deep, powerful convulsions that spasmed around his penis, drawing his own climax from him seconds later.

Marcus groaned and shuddered, his head dipping so that his lips were pressed against her rubber-clad shoulder. As soon as their combined flesh stopped pulsing, Eleanor pushed him away and struggled to get up. Re-fastening the press studs over her burning sex, she stood up and regarded him coldly.

'Now analyse *that*,' she snapped, making no concessions to his momentary exhaustion.

Marcus looked at her, his dark eyes only slowly clearing as he realised that she was still angry, still hurt, that what had happened between them was her revenge on him for abusing her.

'Eleanor . . . we have to talk about this—'

'Talk to yourself, Marcus. If you really want to know what I think about tonight, and about you, then I suggest you read the next chapter of the book, hot off the printer tomorrow. Until then, you'll have to speculate, won't you? And believe me, I can guarantee that this time, you'll have got it one hundred per cent *wrong*.' With that she spun on her heel and stalked out of the door.

# *Chapter Seven*

---

*IN CONCLUSION, I* have discovered that, when the urge is strong, it is perfectly possible for a woman to have sex with a man simply because he is available, without the restriction of needing to know or even like him. When aroused, her sexuality heightened by an evening of stimulation, like a long, drawn-out foreplay of the mind, a woman can use the nearest available man to bring herself relief.

Given the virtual knee-jerk sexual response of the male of the species, it is not hard to find a willing partner.'

Eleanor printed out the final pages of her journal, aware that she would probably rewrite it at a later date. Right now, she was driven by a desire to put Marcus in his place, to shake him out of the smug complacency which seemed to characterise his attitude to female sexuality.

As for what had happened between them – contrary to expectation, she found she had no feelings towards him whatsoever. That part of her narrative, at least, was absolutely true – Marcus had merely been an available cock to satisfy her.

Eleanor grimaced at the crudity of the thought. She never used to think in such terms. Leaving her manuscript pages on Marcus's desk, she took herself off for a long walk in the fresh air.

When she returned at one o'clock, her mind was clearer and she felt physically refreshed. Going up to her room, she showered and changed into fresh clothes before going down to join Marcus for lunch.

She could tell from the expression on his face that he had read her latest contribution to the book, but he made no reference to it whatsoever. He was distant, though, and Eleanor sensed she had angered him. Too bad! she thought to herself. She was still angry at the way he had manipulated her last night, and she was glad that she had been able to redress the balance a little.

'I think I'm ready now to go on to "dominance and submission",' she told him when they were eating dessert.

Marcus looked startled, as if he thought she meant here and now.

'The next chapter?' she reminded him. 'I'm ready to move on.'

His eyes narrowed as he regarded her.

'Yes, I think you're probably right,' he said at last with an edge to his voice. 'In fact, I was discussing the next chapter with Jeanette.'

'Oh?' Remembering the girl in the feathers, Eleanor was cool.

'Yes. She has a friend who supplies dominant services – for a fee. If you're agreeable, she might be willing to take you on as an assistant for a day.'

If Marcus was expecting her to be offended at his suggestion that she turn prostitute for the day, he was sorely disappointed, for Eleanor merely raised her eyebrows at him.

'I see. Have you organised anything yet?'

'As a matter of fact, Cara is calling by this afternoon to meet you.'

Eleanor smiled coolly.

'Good. I'd like to move on as quickly as possible.'

Pushing away her empty plate, she rose.

'Eleanor?'

She glanced at Marcus expectantly, sensing that, for once, he was having difficulty finding the right words to express himself.

'About last night—'

'I think that's a case of least said, soonest mended, don't you?' she interrupted him firmly. 'It's not as if it's likely to happen again.'

Marcus raised an eyebrow at her.

'Are you so sure?'

Eleanor gazed at him, unwilling to acknowledge, even to herself, that he was right – there probably would be a next time.

'Are you?' she countered briskly. 'Now, if you'll excuse me, I want to do a little background reading before I meet this Cara.' She left the room, conscious of Marcus's eyes following her, sensing his frustration.

It wasn't that she'd stopped wanting him, she mused as she went up to her room. Though last night she had used him, it had been good between them. However, over the past few weeks as she had expanded her experience, her confidence had grown. She no longer feared that she could become dependent on him and she was aware that, with a man like Marcus, it was crucial to remain on top of the situation if she was to retain her sanity.

In her room, Eleanor browsed through the magazine she had found on sado-masochism. It was largely concerned with corporal punishment and carried endless photographs of overblown young women in ill-fitting school uniforms and long, repetitive accounts of spankings which were remarkable only for their obsessive attention to detail.

There was another magazine, this time taken up with shots of leather-clad, stony-featured women with a penchant for strutting around in spike-heeled boots. Was this what domination was all about? Eleanor had a feeling that this was going to be the least appealing part of her research to date.

Cara, when she arrived, was a surprise. After flicking through the second magazine, Eleanor had half expected a beefy-looking blonde, probably with a music-hall Germanic accent, dressed in a storm trooper's outfit. Cara, however, although blonde, was petite and slim, her unmade-up face attractively freckled and her slender body dressed in jeans and a fresh-looking white shirt with double cuffs.

'Hello,' she said, holding out her hand.

Eleanor felt the strength in her grip and immediately revised her first impression that the girl was probably as fragile as she looked.

'Pleased to meet you, Cara. It's very kind of you to offer to, er, show me the ropes!'

Cara laughed, a light, natural sound that made Eleanor warm to her.

'I'm sure we'll have a lot of fun together. The only thing I have to ask you is that you be absolutely discreet. You'd be surprised at the identities of some of my regulars!'

'I have a feeling I'll be surprised by more than that!' Eleanor commented ruefully. 'Did Marcus explain that I'm a bit . . . inexperienced in these things?'

Cara smiled, her eyes running quickly over Eleanor, as if weighing up her potential.

'All you have to do is follow my lead – you'll get the idea in no time. Now, do you have time to come into town with me? We'll have to get you kitted out.'

144

'Sure – I'm entirely in your hands, Cara. You lead and I'll follow!'

Cara gave her a quick look, the meaning of which Eleanor simply couldn't fathom. Then she grinned and picked up her bag and the odd expression was gone.

'Time to shop!'

Cara's idea of shopping was quite different to Eleanor's, though what she had expected she couldn't really say. What she hadn't anticipated was that they would spend the afternoon cocooned in the slightly surreal world of a sex shop.

Pandora's Box was tucked away along a side street just outside the main shopping centre. From the outside, its painted windows and discreet sign made it look like just another respectable Victorian terrace, no different from those on either side. Once through the door, though, it was like entering another world.

Sapphire-blue, satin curtains were draped across the top of a steep flight of stairs leading downwards. The stairs were so small that Eleanor had to concentrate on walking down them, clinging onto the rickety bannister as she followed Cara into what seemed like the bowels of the earth.

Only she would not have expected the bowels of the earth to be decorated like the room she reached at the bottom. Swathes of jewel-bright fabrics lined the walls and ceiling like the interior of an emperor's tent, dazzling the eye and creating an intimate, womblike effect in the small space. Along every wall were rack upon rack of clothes, interspersed by shelves displaying every conceivable kind of sex toy and marital aid.

'Cara – good to see you, darling!'

Eleanor turned to see a small, middle-aged woman dressed in a bright purple kaftan, her dark, slightly greying hair pulled back into an untidy bun. As she embraced Cara her bright, dark eyes surveyed Eleanor over her shoulder. After a moment's perusal, her face broke into a beaming smile.

'Introduce me to your lovely friend,' she demanded.

'This is Eleanor. Eleanor – Pandora Green.'

Eleanor stepped forward and offered her hand. The older woman enclosed it in both of hers.

'Welcome to Pandora's Box, my dear!'

Eleanor smiled, responding to the mischievous sparkle in Pandora's eyes.

'Now – what can I help you with?'

Glancing at Cara, Eleanor grimaced.

'To be honest, I'm not too sure.'

'Eleanor is going to *assist* me,' Cara said with a definite smile in her voice. 'She'll need to look the part . . . How about this?'

She picked up a black PVC catsuit with a shiny, wet-look finish.

'Er . . . no, I don't think so,' Eleanor said, eyeing

the outfit with distaste. 'I think I'd suffer from claustrophobia in that!'

Pandora laughed and, running her eyes professionally over Eleanor's body, she picked a selection of clothes for her to try.

'Now, take my advice and get dressed with your back to the mirror. If you watch yourself transforming, bit by bit, it'll put you off. Don't look until you're fully kitted out – then see what you think!'

Pandora handed Eleanor a small pile of clothes and she and Cara went to catch up on news while Eleanor changed.

In the small cubicle, Eleanor stripped off her clothes and looked through the garments Pandora had given her. Everything was made of leather, PVC or rubber, none of which she normally wore. Discarding a red leather dress and an electric blue pair of shiny PVC trousers, Eleanor opted for black.

The skirt she chose was rubberised, lined with white silk that clung to her hips like a second skin. Though it was short, barely reaching mid-thigh, it was too tight for briefs to be a viable proposition, so she opted for sleek black tights instead. It wasn't until she pulled them up that she realised that there was a split at the crotch, strategically placed to leave her sex exposed.

With a small shrug of resignation, Eleanor pushed her feet into the spiky-heeled ankle boots trimmed with maribou feathers and turned her attention to the top half of her. Deciding that chainmail simply wasn't her, and that she couldn't quite bring herself to wear silver lurex, she was left with a supple leather waistcoat which, when she fastened it, gave her an impressive cleavage.

Only now, slowly, did she turn to meet her reflection in the cubicle's full-length mirror.

'Oh my God!' she said aloud.

'Let's see.' Cara pulled back the curtain and Eleanor turned to face them. 'Wow! You look terrific!'

'I look like a tart.'

'As Cara said – you look terrific,' Pandora said, smiling. 'Look again.'

Eleanor turned reluctantly towards the mirror and surveyed her reflection. She had to admit, she looked like the stereotypical view of every man's dream woman, oozing sexuality with a hint of knowingness.

'I do look . . . different,' she said cautiously.

'More powerful,' Cara added.

'I suppose so, yes,' Eleanor said, surprised to realise the adjective was exactly right. 'More powerful. Dressed like this, I could drive a man wild!'

Cara laughed, delighted by Eleanor's response.

'And you will, Eleanor, I promise you. This Friday, ten o'clock. I'll take your gear back with me, then you can change at my place.'

Eleanor nodded, aware that she was beginning

to look forward to this next stage in her research. For if she could feel like this merely by dressing up in these outlandish clothes, what would she feel like when she was given power over a real, living, breathing man?

Cara lived in a spacious Victorian terrace decorated in Laura Ashley prints and sparsely, though tastefully, furnished with antiques sympathetic to the period of the house. It was not what Eleanor had expected from a woman who earned her crust as a dominatrix.

As before, Cara herself was wearing jeans and a shirt, her pretty face bare of make-up and her blonde hair pulled back into a ponytail.

'Hi – I'm glad you're on time. That means we've got time for a coffee.'

She showed Eleanor through to a large high-ceilinged kitchen-come-dining room which was filled with sunlight streaming through the large, uncurtained windows.

'Now, I imagine you've got a few questions,' she said when they had settled at the scrubbed pine table with their coffee. 'Fire away!'

Eleanor took a sip of her coffee and smiled.

'To tell you the truth, Cara, I've come with a completely open mind. I might have questions later, but for now I'd rather learn "on the job".'

Cara nodded approvingly.

'Good. In that case, all I have to tell you is to keep quiet and follow my lead. You'll soon get the idea – but don't, whatever you do, break into my clients' fantasies. You'll see what I mean,' she added cryptically.

The doorbell rang then and Cara glanced at her watch.

'That'll be George – he's early!'

'But we haven't even changed yet!' Eleanor said, panicking.

Cara smiled. 'No need for this one. You sit there and enjoy your coffee. Take your time.'

The doorbell rang again and Cara frowned. 'He's impatient today.'

Going over to a long cupboard by the door, she reached in and brought out a riding crop. Laying it where it couldn't be missed on the table, she gave Eleanor a wink before leaving the room.

Eleanor listened as Cara opened the door, hearing, with some surprise, how her voice changed. Gone was the easy-going, musical cadence, replaced by a strong, almost strident tone that didn't sound like her at all.

'What do you mean by ringing the doorbell twice?' she heard her say. 'You're early – how dare you try to rush me!'

'I'm most sorry, Madam,' Eleanor heard a clipped, fawning male voice say, 'I was just so eager to see you . . .'

They walked into the kitchen. Eleanor saw a grey-haired gentleman in late middle age, wearing a smart city suit, carrying a carefully furled black umbrella in one hand and a capacious-looking briefcase in the other. When the man saw Eleanor sitting calmly at the kitchen table, he looked alarmed, his gaze switching to Cara almost fearfully.

'This is Madam Eleanor,' Cara told him. 'Mind your manners now, and go and change.'

She waited until the bemused man had hurried into what Eleanor had assumed was the kitchen pantry before sitting down again and picking up her coffee cup.

'Don't take any notice of George – he's here to clean the kitchen.'

'He's *what*?' Eleanor spluttered.

'Here to clean. Have you never had a slave, Eleanor? I'd recommend it – they're generally very thorough, and free, of course. All it costs me is the occasional thwack across the rump with this.' She picked up the riding crop and swished it through the air. It made a faint whistling sound and Eleanor winced as she imagined it coming down onto bare flesh.

Cara laughed softly at Eleanor's expression.

'Try not to let him see you're shocked. Contempt and ridicule are fine, but shock would make him feel defensive. Ah, here he is now. Do hurry up, George – I want you out of here within the hour.'

'Yes, Madam, of course. I'll start with the surfaces, shall I?'

'Whatever – just snap to it!'

Eleanor gazed at George, who had stripped off

his clothes and was now wearing nothing but his shoes and socks, a plastic apron which did nothing to conceal his nakedness and a headscarf tied around his head like a Forties housewife. It was all Eleanor could do not to burst out laughing, but Cara shot her a warning look and so she concentrated on pouring herself more coffee.

From the corner of her eye, she could see George clearing the kitchen work surface before arming himself with a scouring pad and a cream cleanser. No wonder Cara's kitchen sparkled! she thought to herself, watching him scour the work tops.

As soon as he'd finished, he filled a bucket with soapy water and went down on his hands and knees to scrub the floor. His skinny buttocks waggled furiously as he scrubbed. Cara got up and, with a wicked look at Eleanor, gave him a half-hearted *thwack* across the bottom.

'Put some effort into it, George,' she said. 'Madam Eleanor and I are going downstairs to get changed.'

'But Madam, I thought—'

'Quiet!' she silenced him with a word, ignoring the disappointment written clearly across his face. 'Let yourself out, George, when you've finished, but see to it that you do a good job! If you do, you may come back on Tuesday at ten, and I'll allow you to clean downstairs as well.'

'Oh, thank you, Madam!' George said, his features transformed with joy as he bent his head and pressed his lips against the top of Cara's foot.

Cara bent down and patted him on the top of his head absently, as she might have patted an obedient dog.

'Come on, Eleanor – it's time for us to get changed.'

Eleanor followed Cara out of the kitchen, still bemused by the sight of George, his headscarf slightly awry, scrubbing the kitchen tiles.

'But what pleasure could he possibly get out of that?' she asked.

Cara shrugged. 'I've never really thought about it. I've had George for two years now, before that he was Pandora's.'

'You mean, she passed him on?'

'Something like that.' Cara flashed her a grin. 'George is getting a bit long in the tooth now – Pandora has a guy in his late twenties who isn't averse to straight sex when she fancies it. I can see you're shocked, but it's an ideal arrangement for a single woman. No housework to worry about and sex on tap.'

'I'm sure it is,' Eleanor said faintly.

Cara laughed. 'Wait until you see my dungeon!'

Eleanor realised that the steps down which they were walking lead to the cellar, but she was totally unprepared for the sight which met her eyes as Cara opened the door and stood aside to let her pass.

'What do you think?' she asked, an unmistakable note of pride in her voice.

Eleanor walked in and looked around her. She

was standing in the middle of a large, square room which was painted entirely in black. Black walls, black ceiling, black tiles on the floor. On one wall there was a rack holding a neat array of whips, canes, crops and various manacles. Along one of the longer walls was an arrangement of metal rings embedded into the brickwork.

There was a small handbasin in one corner, the sanitary ware looking incongruously white against the black background. Looking up, Eleanor saw that there was a contraption attached to the ceiling which looked like a pulley. At the end of the room there was a couch, much like those found in hospital examination rooms. Beside the couch was a trolley set with disposable gloves, a jug, a bowl and various lengths of rubber hosing. Eleanor glanced at Cara questioningly.

'Don't worry, I've made sure that today's clients are all fairly straightforward – I thought that too many bodily fluids might put you off.'

'Yes. Um . . . what do I do now?'

Eleanor was aware that she sounded nervous and she took several deep, calming breaths. Walking over to her, Cara gave her shoulder a reassuring squeeze.

'Now we get changed. Don't worry – this is going to be fun! I promise.'

Passing her an uncertain smile, Eleanor followed her into the small changing room concealed behind a door beside the wash basin.

Once they were dressed, Cara passed her a leather eye mask.

'Marcus explained that you wanted to guard your privacy – this will disguise you, and add to the fun for my clients!'

'Who have you got coming?' Eleanor asked as she eased the mask over her eyes. It was surprisingly comfortable, fitting neatly over the bridge of her nose.

'The first one is a Mr Porter. He's a regular, comes for straightforward CP once a month.'

'CP?'

'Corporal punishment. Pretty tired stuff.' Cara smiled wickedly and crammed her hair up into a mortarboard.

She was wearing a tight rubber mini-dress which outlined every curve of her perfectly proportioned figure. Her legs were encased in black fishnet tights and rubberised boots which reached to mid thigh. While they were talking, she quickly made up her face, so that by the time they were both ready, she was virtually unrecognisable as the fresh-faced young girl who had greeted Eleanor at the door.

'Are you ready?' Cara asked her.

'As ready as I'll ever be!' Eleanor admitted.

'You'll be fine. You look good anyway,' Cara added, holding her head on one side as she ran her eyes over Eleanor from top to toe. 'Good enough to eat!' she added.

Once again, Eleanor felt a small *frisson* of

155

excitement, tinged with alarm. There was no time to dwell on it though, for as Cara opened the cellar door, they heard George let himself out, just before the doorbell rang.

'Wait here,' Cara said as she went slowly up the stairs to let her client in.

Eleanor didn't quite know what to do with herself. In the end, she opted to lurk in the shadows in the corner of the room, wanting to see and weigh up Cara's client before he saw her. Mr Porter, when he appeared, was a small, nervous-looking man with a smooth, boyish face which went uneasily with his elderly body.

'Madam Eleanor!'

Eleanor snapped to attention as Cara called her and she stepped out into the pool of light shed by the single, unshaded lightbulb.

'Y-yes, Madam Cara?' Aware that she sounded unacceptably timid, she cleared her throat and repeated herself more firmly. Cara nodded at her approvingly.

'I found this . . . pipsqueak,' she said, nudging the man with the tip of her forefinger contemptuously, 'skulking outside on the doorstep. What did you think you were doing, Porter?' she barked.

The man cowered away from her, but Eleanor noticed that his eyes were bright, watching Cara's face avidly. There was a thin covering of sweat on his upper lip and he was breathing rapidly, through his mouth.

'I'm sorry, Miss,' he said fawningly.

156

'Sorry isn't good enough,' Cara sneered. 'What do you think, Madam Eleanor – six of the best?'

'Oh . . . at least!' Eleanor replied gamely.

'You hear that, Porter? My colleague thinks you deserve more than six!'

The man paled slightly, though he nodded his head.

'Oh yes,' he said eagerly, 'if Miss thinks so!'

'Go and chose a cane then, you miserable boy.'

Mr Porter scurried over to the rack and took his time selecting a long, bamboo cane. Eleanor watched in bemusement as he picked up a long, springy example and touched it almost reverently to his lips before passing it to Cara.

'Right. Trousers down and over the chair.'

As she spoke, Cara drew out an old-fashioned wooden chair and positioned it in the middle of the room. Eleanor felt like a spare part, until Cara directed her to stand beside the hapless Mr Porter, so that she would have a grandstand view of the proceedings.

Waiting until he was lying across the chair, his trousers and underpants pooled around his knees, Cara swished the cane through the air theatrically. Mr Porter trembled, his buttocks, very white under the glare of the bulb, shivering with either cold or anticipation.

Eleanor stared at Cara, who gave her an exaggerated wink. The cane sang through the air and landed across the lower part of his buttocks, neatly striping the point where his thighs and buttocks met. Eleanor's sharp intake of breath matched Mr Porter's. Cara raised her arm again and brought the cane about an inch above the original site.

'The trick,' she told Eleanor as she waited for Mr Porter to regain his breath, 'is to make sure that the cane never touches the same line twice. We're aiming for a series of neat, thin red lines, no broken skin. Isn't that right, Porter?'

'Oh yes, Miss,' he gasped, clenching his buttocks as he sensed that she was about to administer another blow.

Eleanor winced as the third was swiftly followed by two more.

'What have we got to, Madam Eleanor?' Cara asked.

'Er . . . five,' she answered.

'One more should suffice for today I think.'

Cara was perspiring and Eleanor noticed she was slightly out of breath as she striped Mr Porter's buttocks just below the tail of his spine. This was clearly hard physical work, which accounted for Cara's strength.

'Could you apply the salve?' she asked Eleanor, nodding towards a large pot of cream on the shelf.

Eleanor said nothing, but she brought down the jar and opened it. Mr Porter was still lying prone across the chair, his buttocks no longer white but a flaming red. Could she bear to touch him? Fighting down her instinctive distaste,

Eleanor scooped out a generous amount of the cooling cream and slathered it across the wretched man's buttocks.

His skin felt hot, burning against her palm as she smoothed the cream across his flesh. Mr Porter moaned, though it seemed to Eleanor that it was more with pleasure than with pain.

When she had finished, she turned to Cara, who had been watching her closely. She smiled.

'Good. Wash your hands while I see Mr Porter out.'

Mr Porter was already dressing, gathering his dignity as he fastened his clothes. Though he walked a little stiffly, there was little trace of the excited, cringing individual who had walked in. Cara treated him accordingly, fussing over him and taking his money at the door.

'Well?' she said as she came back downstairs and began washing her hands. 'What did you think?'

'I'm totally perplexed!' Eleanor admitted. 'What on earth was that all about? I mean, he didn't even have an erection, never mind ejaculate – what on earth did he get out of it?'

'It's a common misconception that men who like to be beaten tie their obsession in with a climax. There are many like Mr Porter, who get their kicks through physical pain – it doesn't have to have much to do with sex. The atmosphere, the direction of a Mistress and the actual punishment itself is enough.'

'How can you bear it? I mean – it's enough to put you off men for life!'

Cara gave her an odd look. 'I've never been that keen anyway. There are an awful lot of submissive men out there, Eleanor, far more than most people realise. We've got time for a quick coffee before the next caning.'

Over coffee, Eleanor questioned Cara more.

'You did very well, by the way,' Cara told her. 'If you'd like to get gradually more involved with each client, I've booked in someone rather special for our last appointment – someone we can have a bit of fun with!'

Intrigued, Eleanor asked her to elaborate, but Cara would not be drawn, merely smiling enigmatically whenever Eleanor mentioned their final appointment. Over the following hours, they saw three more men, on whom Eleanor practised her fledgling whipping skills.

The first time she picked up a cane and brought it down across bare flesh, she did it with little conviction, wincing as she imagined herself administering pain. Gradually, though, she realised that her enthusiasm for her task was part of the unspoken contract between herself and the client and she tried harder.

There was something rather satisfying about the precision required when striping white skin with bands of pink. It was made easy by the fact that the men were mere faceless ciphers to her, a pair of buttocks waiting to be warmed or, in the

160

case of one man, a body to be wrapped in Sellotape which was then slowly peeled off.

By the time the final client was due, Eleanor was tired and hot and almost as blasé as Cara. Then the client walked into the room and, suddenly, all her weariness disappeared.

He was gorgeous – six feet two, early thirties, slim and healthy-looking. His hair was short and a glossy brown, his jaw square with an attractive cleft in the centre. Eleanor would never have taken him for a submissive, but for the way he looked at her, shyly from beneath his long, dark eyelashes.

'This is Tod,' Cara told her, caressing his arm lazily through the thin shirt he wore. 'He's less of a client, more of a friend, so we can take our time. Enjoy ourselves, maybe. Goodness knows, we deserve it!' she said, rolling her eyes at Eleanor. 'Meet Eleanor, Tod.'

Tod smiled, showing perfectly straight, white teeth, and enclosed her hand in his. His grip was strong and confident, and Eleanor found herself responding to him.

'Pleased to meet you, Tod,' she said, aware that he was looking deeply into her eyes, which were partially obscured by the eye mask. 'Um . . . why are you here?'

He laughed and shrugged.

'I like playing games,' he explained. 'When I'm between girlfriends I come to Cara.'

'Okay, that's enough talk,' Cara said briskly. 'Strip off your clothes, Tod, and lie on the bed.'

161

Eleanor watched in amazement as with a quick, almost shy smile in her direction, Tod immediately removed all his clothes and lay down as instructed on the couch. He had a well-moulded, smooth body, evenly tanned. His cock was straight and strong-looking, lying semi-erect against his belly.

Cara smiled at him and picked up a blindfold.

'Close your eyes, darling,' she cooed as she tied it around his head.

Glancing across at Eleanor, she indicated that she should pick a selection of manacles from the rack. Then she secured each of his wrists and ankles in turn, so that he was lying spread-eagled on the examination couch.

Eleanor was aware that she found the sight of him, naked, bound and helpless, rather arousing. He had a beautiful body, it was true, but she knew that it was not that which was moving her, but his vulnerability. Tied and blindfolded, he was completely at their mercy.

Cara caught her eye at the very moment when she acknowledged her own growing excitement. She smiled at her, beckoning her over with a crooked finger and offering her a bottle of oil. Touching a finger to her lip to indicate that silence should be maintained, she mimed that Eleanor should massage the oil over Tod's upper body.

Eleanor took the bottle, but did not act immediately. Instead, she stood at his head, looking down at his body, and waited, watching

162

how he tensed, all his senses alert as he wondered what was going on. Gradually, his muscles tautened to the point where Eleanor knew he was ready to fight or take flight, and she could sense the rush of adrenalin through his veins. Only then, when she had eked out the tension for as long as possible, did she lift the bottle high and trickle the thick, oily fluid over his chest and belly.

Tod jumped at the first contact of the cold oil against his skin, his breath emerging on a small hiss of surprise. Putting the bottle aside, Eleanor flexed her fingers and, leaning over him, began to massage the oil into his chest.

Cara nodded at her and, picking up the oil, went to massage his feet. The two women worked in silence, oiling him carefully all over. Eleanor could feel the rubbery points of his nipples brushing against her palms as she worked over the steady thud of his heartbeat. His skin felt smooth and warm, responding to the tactile pleasure by rising up in small goosebumps.

Eleanor felt as she had when Lars had been presented to her – totally in control. It was a powerful feeling, arousing her in a way that was deep and satisfying. The young man bound to the couch trembled beneath her touch as she stroked his skin, mirroring Cara's movements at the other end of the couch.

'How do you feel, darling?' Cara said after a while.

'Wonderful,' Tod admitted, 'but won't you take off the blindfold? I'd love to be able to look at you both.'

'All in good time,' Cara replied mildly. 'First I want to warm you up a little.'

He shuddered with anticipation as Cara fetched two small many-fronded whips from the rack. Passing one to Eleanor, she showed her how to fasten it onto her wrist with a loop, so that the main body of the handle was held at the base of her palm.

Tod gasped as Cara flicked the leather tendrils across his thighs in a sweeping motion. Eleanor followed suit, working her way across his chest and down to his belly with small, flicking motions. It wasn't hard enough to be significantly painful, but it was bracing enough to bring the blood to the surface of his skin, turning it pink.

She noticed that his cock had risen in response to the intense stimulation, and she couldn't resist trailing the ends of the fronds along it, noticing how he squirmed with anticipation. Cara shook her head.

'Use this,' she said.

'This' was an odd-looking contraption, like a harness, made of leather, which Eleanor soon realised was designed to slip over the penis, flattening it down as the strap was buckled around his waist.

'You're too cruel, Cara,' Tod moaned, clearly loving every minute.

'*Now* I think we'll take off the blindfold,' she said, ignoring him.

It wasn't until Tod's eyes were following them slavishly as they walked together round the bed that Eleanor realised quite how exquisite a 'punishment' Cara was meting out. Strapped to the bed, his cock subdued by the leather harness, Tod could only look, not touch.

Smiling at her, Cara reached towards Eleanor and unfastened the top button of her leather waistcoat.

'Mmm . . . Give Tod a peek at these, darling,' she said, running the tip of her finger lightly along the line of her cleavage.

Feeling out of her depth suddenly, Eleanor went obediently to lean over Tod so that he could look down the front of her waistcoat at her bare breasts.

'Aren't they lovely, Tod?' Cara was saying, making Eleanor supremely self-conscious. She looked round in surprise as the dungeon door opened and Jeanette stepped inside.

Cara went over to her and the two women embraced. Then, to Eleanor's intense discomfort, they kissed deeply, their bodies entwining as naturally as any lovers of long standing.

'You've met Jeanette, haven't you?' Cara asked when they finally broke apart.

'Of course,' Eleanor replied, at a loss to know what to do. 'It was at the club.'

Jeanette smiled at her and, striding across the room, kissed her on both cheeks.

'We didn't get time to talk in the club, Eleanor, which is why I've gatecrashed today – I'd love to get to know you better!'

Eleanor was aware that she was very conscious of the light scent of Jeanette's perfume and of the softness of her skin as she pressed her cheek against hers. She'd never noticed another woman in that way before, and the unexpected awareness confused her.

'Pretty,' Jeanette commented, turning her attention to Tod. 'Is it nice and tight?' she flicked the cock harness negligently with one long fingernail, making Tod groan.

'Yes,' he replied through gritted teeth as his nerve endings protested.

'Good. You can relax for a while now,' she told him, slowly peeling off her coat to reveal that she was naked underneath it. 'Cara and I want to play with Eleanor for a while. If you turn your head to one side, you're welcome to watch. Eleanor's going to try a little mild S & M herself – isn't that right, Eleanor?'

Eleanor gaped at her. At once the cellar seemed claustrophobic, the black walls and ceiling closing in on her, making it difficult to breathe.

'What?' she whispered.

Cara came up behind her and slipped her arms around her waist.

'It's a little surprise – we thought you might welcome a new experience.'

'But . . . no thank you, I wouldn't like it! It

doesn't appeal to me at all.'

Even as she said the words, Eleanor knew she was lying. The idea of these two beautiful women tying her up and tormenting her as she had so recently been tormenting Tod sent an unmistakeable *frisson* zinging through her veins.

Jeanette was watching her closely. 'I think you *would* like it, darling. I promise we won't really hurt you, just tease you a little. If at any time you want us to stop, you only have to say so.'

'Do say yes, Eleanor,' Cara said softly. 'It would be such fun!' As she spoke, her long fingers were gently circling her nipples encased in the leather waistcoat.

Swallowing, Eleanor opened her mouth and heard her own voice emerging, as if from far away.

'All right,' it said, and she knew that she was lost.

# Chapter Eight

THEY TIED HER with silk scarves so that her arms were pulled apart at shoulder level, bent upwards at the elbow and secured at the wrists to the rings embedded in the ceiling. Eleanor was conscious that the gentle restraint was not unpleasant, that there was something almost liberating about being placed in position like this. She felt as if she was abdicating all responsibility for her own body, handing over to them the burden of care.

She protested slightly when Cara knelt at her feet and fastened a thin metal bar between her ankles which forced her legs apart.

'I don't think—'

'Ssh! Trust me,' Cara said, her voice resonating with suppressed desire. 'It will be better this way.'

Eleanor realised that there was something

dangerously thrilling about having her legs forced apart like this and held in position, but the logical side of her brain still protested.

'Please, I'm not happy with—' Jeanette silenced her, most effectively, by kissing her.

Eleanor had never been kissed by another woman before, and at first she instinctively resisted the pressure applied, and the instant rush of pleasure that followed. She gritted her teeth and held her lips rigid, rejecting the teasing probe of the other woman's questing tongue.

It was useless. Jeanette's lips were soft and sweet-tasting, coaxing her own apart. Eleanor responded with a small sound of distress as her mouth opened under the gently insistent pressure of the other woman's and admitted her tongue.

Jeanette probed softly, putting her arms around Eleanor and pressing her against the firm, curvaceous contours of her own body.

'Relax,' she murmured as she broke away. 'Allow yourself to enjoy.'

Eleanor stared at her, wide-eyed. Though the kiss had been pleasurable, though every muscle and sinew now trembled with anticipation, her inherent discomfort with anything non-heterosexual held her back.

'I've never done this before. I'm not a lesbian,' she protested feebly as Cara began to unfasten her waistcoat.

Jeanette smiled at her as if understanding her dilemma.

'You don't have to be a lesbian to enjoy yourself with other women. You're safe here – forget yourself for a while, Eleanor.'

'Go with the flow!' Cara interjected softly.

'That's right. And afterwards we'll send you back to the man in your life with a new dimension, so you'll have even more to give . . .'

*The man in her life?* Eleanor thought of Rhys and what he would make of this. Would he understand? *Does it matter?* A small voice in her head asked her. After all, though she hoped he would benefit in the long run, this was primarily for her and her alone.

'This is for you,' Jeanette murmured in her ear, unwittingly echoing her tangled thoughts.

Eleanor shivered as Cara bent down and enclosed one tumid nipple in her hot mouth. Gathering up the whole breast in one hand, she flicked the centre with her tongue, sending tremors of delight through Eleanor's entire body. Her mouth was so soft, her teeth grazing lightly over the sensitised flesh of her areolae, making her gasp.

As Cara worked on her breasts, her mouth at one while she caressed the other with her fingers, Jeanette moved behind her and traced the outline of her bottom in the tight, rubberised skirt with her hands. Eleanor was aware of her body responding, blossoming like a flower under the women's combined caresses.

Glancing across at Tod, still spread-eagled on

170

the bed, she saw that he was watching her. Their eyes met and held and Eleanor recognised her own need reflected in his. Both were at the mercy of these two women, both craved release and had reached the stage where they would do anything to get it.

'Oh!' Eleanor gasped as Jeanette eased her skirt up over her waist and traced her fingertips round the seam of the open-crotch tights.

Curling her fingers round the edge, she eased them apart so that her entire vulva was exposed. As if at a hidden signal, Cara stopped kissing and sucking at her breasts and stood up. Eleanor saw that her features seemed blurred by her own pleasure and she strained forward, wanting to give in to the sudden urge to kiss the other girl on the mouth.

Cara allowed her to touch her lips in a kiss all too brief, then she moved away. She smiled as she produced a blindfold and advanced. Eleanor panicked.

'I don't want you to whip or beat me,' she said emphatically.

'Of course not, darling,' Jeanette said from behind her.

Reaching round to stroke her breasts for a moment, she slipped the waistcoat off her shoulders before taking the blindfold from Cara.

'There's more than one way to play this game,' she whispered enigmatically.

Eleanor closed her eyes as the blindfold

blocked out the light. She felt almost frighteningly exposed, vulnerable in a way she had never felt before. Imagining how she looked, naked from the waist up with just a rucked-up skirt around her middle and the ruins of her tights around her knees, she felt doubly exposed. It was worse, somehow, than being completely naked. More shameful.

'All right?' Cara murmured and, despite her reservations, Eleanor nodded.

Having worked with Cara all afternoon, she knew she was in the hands of an expert, even though it seemed now that it was Jeanette who was calling all the shots.

It was Jeanette who reached round her now and covered her breasts with her warm, oil-covered hands. In much the same way as Eleanor had worked in tandem with Cara, now Cara and Jeanette worked together to oil and prepare Eleanor's body for – what? Eleanor shivered, not so much with fear, though she was afraid, but with excitement.

The sweet, almond-scented perfume of the oil hung heavily in the air, making her feel quite dizzy. Something in it made her skin tingle and grow warm, until eventually she felt as if she was glowing all over. The warmth reached into her, so that she could imagine the source of the glow was within, radiating outward.

Would they go against her wishes and whip her? Eleanor shuddered at the thought, instinctively aware that she would not enjoy any kind of physical pain. As both women stood back for a moment, she tensed, half expecting a blow. The soft brush against her skin took her by surprise.

'What is that?' she said.

'Ssh.'

The object stroked down from her collarbones, between her breasts, and swirled around her navel. It felt like – like a feather. The most exquisite sensations trickled through her as Jeanette began to stroke her from behind with another feather. Her body felt light, almost weightless as they stroked her in a choreographed pattern, so softly she wondered if she was going to be able to bear it. Not quite a tickle, but close enough to it for Eleanor to virtually hold her breath in anticipation.

Her breasts hardened, her nipples cresting into two aching little peaks as the tip of one feather was swirled around them. She heard Tod groan and imagined his cock rising against the cruel restraint of the harness, aching to be free.

'Let me untie you, Tod,' she heard Cara say. 'Do you have any objection, Eleanor?'

Eleanor thought of the contrast of the firm, masculine body against the softness of the two women and shook her head. She felt as if she was on fire, the entire surface area of her skin sensitised beyond endurance by the feathers they had used to stroke and tease her.

She moaned softly as Jeanette's fingers moved

delicately over her labia, knowing that they were swollen and moist. As Jeanette stroked them, they opened, welcoming her fingers in, and Eleanor gave a small sob of submission as she entered her with two fingers.

'Beautiful,' Jeanette murmured against her hair, 'so warm and lovely. I'd like to lick you, Eleanor, I'd like to press my tongue in here and taste the sweetness of you.'

'Oh! No . . . I . . .'

'But I know you'd prefer it to be a male tongue. Pity. Luckily though we've got a willing male right here. On your knees, Tod darling.'

Eleanor tensed as she sensed Tod kneeling in front of her. She could feel his warm breath against her thighs, could hear the way he tried to control his ragged breathing.

'No hands now, Tod,' Cara commanded him, 'just your lips and tongue.'

Eleanor heard the soft whistle of a whip through the air followed by Tod's sharp intake of breath as it landed across his back. He leaned forward and touched the apex of her labia oh-so delicately with the tip of his tongue.

'That's good, Tod,' Cara purred, her long fingers stroking idly down the slope of Eleanor's breast. 'Nice and slow . . .'

'How does it feel, Eleanor?' Jeanette asked, her voice caressing her, adding to the building tension.

'Good,' Eleanor admitted as Tod's tongue slid

along the swollen folds of flesh towards the entrance to her body.

The leg-spreader held her legs apart at a set distance, thwarting her desire to edge her feet outward. Instead, she wriggled her hips, tilting up her pelvis to give him access to the silky passageway, which ached and wept with need.

Gone was the reluctance, the denial – in their place was a raging, all-consuming desire that swept away every inhibition in its path. At that moment, Eleanor knew, it did not matter if the tongue that pleasured her belonged to a man or a woman, it only mattered that it should not stop.

Tod's tongue was stiff and insistent, sliding into her, bringing his nose against the burning promontory of her clitoris. Eleanor's breath began to hurt in her chest as her heart raced in time with the pulse beating between her legs. Perspiration ran between her breasts and down her sides, mixing with the oil that was still to be absorbed by her skin.

'I'm going to remove the blindfold now.'

Eleanor barely registered Jeanette's words; she had withdrawn into a deeper sensual realm, beginning the inexorable journey towards orgasm. She blinked as the darkness eased, taking some time to refocus her eyes.

Jeanette went to take Cara into her arms and, with a seductive smile in Eleanor's direction, began to kiss her. Jeanette held Eleanor's eye as she plundered the other girl's mouth, their

175

expression challenging her not to find the sight arousing.

Eleanor could not deny that it was. Cara, slender and fair, her deceptively fragile-looking body bent over Jeanette's arm, was a perfect foil for the darker, sturdier Jeanette. No less beautiful, but more statuesque, she held Cara almost protectively, capitalising on the aura of control that surrounded her.

Aesthetically speaking, the sight of the two women kissing so passionately was quite lovely, providing a pleasant spur to Eleanor's race to climax. But it was the man on his knees in front of her who provided the focus to her passion.

Tod was working tirelessly at the sensitive folds between her thighs, his expression rapt as he licked and nipped and sucked at her quivering flesh. His cock, still bound cruelly at his belly, had swollen to the point where Eleanor knew that the constriction must be causing him pain, for the criss-crossed leather thongs that made up the harness were biting into the flesh of his shaft.

Cara must have realised this too, for she broke away from Jeanette and released him before resuming their embrace. Eleanor felt Tod's gasp of relief as his penis sprang free and she bore down against his lips.

The scenes being enacted around her: the two women kissing and caressing each other with growing passion; the man kneeling at her feet, pleasuring her with his mouth whilst moving the

176

skin back and forth over his penis with his own hand; the thought of herself bound and oiled, helpless in the face of such relentless seduction – all these things took on a surreal quality, making her feel as though she was an actor in some weird and structureless play.

Yet, in another way, it made perfect sense. Her body certainly thought the situation ideal. Rushing headlong towards climax, Eleanor cried out, bucking her hips and mashing her pelvis against Tod's face. The black-painted dungeon seemed to disintegrate before her eyes into a swirling kaleidoscope of colour.

As if from far away, Eleanor heard Tod gasp as he reached his own crisis and she sagged against the silk scarves that bound her, mind and body closing down as she sought to contain the maelstrom of sensation that rioted through her.

Then all grew silent, save the sound of her own breathing, intermingling with the laboured panting coming from Tod, and the sighs and gasps of the two women as they sank together onto the cellar floor.

Eleanor felt vaguely dissatisfied as she walked back to the house. After they had released her, Cara, Jeanette and Tod had been so unnervingly matter-of-fact about the whole affair that Eleanor felt quite disorientated. Obviously, such encounters were commonplace to each of them, but to her the experience had been a one-off, an aid to her self-education that, though she had enjoyed it at the time, she didn't think she would want to repeat.

It all seemed so cold, somehow. The fact that she had been able to react at all was testament to how far she had come using the 'retraining' techniques Marcus was exploring. She acknowledged that she was able to enjoy the sensual experience, but felt curiously bereft without the involvement of her heart and mind.

That was what was missing. Sex was all very well, but one had to feel *involved*. Eager to discuss this with Marcus, Eleanor quickened her pace.

As soon as she let herself into the house, Eleanor sensed that all was not as it should be. It was quiet, for a start, which was unusual at this time of the day when Marcus was normally finishing work for the day and Maggie was preparing dinner.

She knew he was in, because his hire car was parked in its usual spot outside. Perhaps he was changing before dinner? Deciding to let him know she was back, Eleanor ran lightly up the stairs. Dropping her bag and jacket into her own room, she then continued along the landing to Marcus's.

Her steps faltered as she approached and she heard an unmistakable sound through the half-opened door. A woman's sigh, low and redolent with passion. Eleanor considered turning back to her own room, but curiosity got the

178

better of her, keeping her where she was. Who on earth could Marcus have in there with him?

Edging towards the door, Eleanor found she could see almost the entire room reflected in the dressing-table mirror which was angled in such a way that she could see it from the door. Marcus was standing at the end of the bed, his eyes half closed, his head thrown back. From his expression and the fine film of perspiration on his forehead, Eleanor guessed that he was near to coming – and no wonder, for, kneeling at his feet with his cock in her mouth, was the housekeeper, Maggie.

Suppressing the initial dart of shock, Eleanor found herself taking in every small detail of the scene. Maggie was naked, her dark hair loose, flowing over her shoulders to cover her breasts. It fell forward to conceal her expression, but she gave every appearance of enjoying fellating him, her body undulating in time with the movement of her head.

Eleanor could see the fine sculpture of her spine from the nape of her neck to her tail. Her body was slim and pale, the skin almost translucent in the daylight, peppered with freckles.

Marcus too was naked. It was the first time Eleanor had seen him without his clothes and she liked what she could see. His chest was broad and nicely defined, lightly furred with dark, silky-looking hair. He looked stronger than he did when his body was covered; his biceps bulging as he tensed in the throes of orgasm.

He opened his mouth on a shuddering sigh as he came. Eleanor felt her own sex-flesh stir in empathy as she gazed at the expression on his face. It was one of pure bliss, transforming his features from ordinary handsomeness to true beauty.

Maggie reached up to hold him by the buttocks as she swallowed his emission, her eyes closed, as if receiving a benediction.

Then, as Eleanor watched, Marcus opened his eyes and looked straight at her in the mirror. Their eyes met and held, his dark and smouldering, hers wide and excited. There was no need for words, they communicated by look alone.

*Later*, his eyes said to her. *Yes*, she signalled back, and by unspoken consent, she withdrew before Maggie saw her. She walked back to her room on shaking legs, stunned by what she had witnessed. It was like an echo of the scene she had stumbled across in Michael's office – someone she cared about making love with someone else. Obviously her feelings for Marcus did not compare with those she had held for her husband, but the principle was the same. Now, as then, she was beset by conflicting emotions. A sense of shock, betrayal, emotional pain, but most of all, a churning excitement.

It was that feeling that she hung onto as she went back to her room to wait for him. That, and a quiet confidence that, this time, she knew exactly what she wanted from him.

## Chapter Nine

*HE DIDN'T MAKE* her wait for long. Eleanor heard Maggie go downstairs, presumably to start the dinner. She wondered, briefly, how long this had been part of the general routine – and how was it that she hadn't noticed? Then she realised that she didn't really care. Marcus was her mentor, her guide through the hitherto unfamiliar territory of sexual experience. She had no claims on him, nor did she want any. But, at that moment at least, she did want him.

'Eleanor,' he began as he walked through her door half an hour later, but she held up her hand to silence him. He looked at her questioningly and she stood up slowly. Holding his eye, she took a step towards him.

'Fuck me, Marcus,' she said.

He looked at her for a long moment.

'Just like that?' he said.

Eleanor smiled faintly. 'What's the matter, Marcus? Are you worried you might have created a monster? We should retitle your book: *From Celibacy To Nymphomania The Marcus Grant Way – How To Learn To Love It*. Or is it just that you're afraid that you can't control the result of your experiments?'

His eyes darkened and she realised that she had angered him. So much the better – she was determined that this time she would elicit some real emotion from him. Even a negative emotion like anger was better than the clinical indifference he normally contrived to display.

'That's not very fair,' he said with infuriating calm.

Eleanor ignored him. She felt hot and restless, her skin prickled and a dull pulse beat an insistent tattoo between her thighs.

'I want you to use all your expertise, all your experience to enable me to put into practice the lessons I've learned over the past few weeks. You said that any woman could "retrain" her sexual responses. Well, here's your chance to test your theory for real.'

'What do you mean?'

'I mean that I've changed, probably beyond recognition. The woman you met at your hotel in London would have run a mile if you'd tried to make a pass at her. Now I'm asking you to fuck me. Thoroughly. Now.'

Marcus advanced into the room. As he came

closer, Eleanor saw that, far from being unaffected by her blunt admission that she wanted him, he was having difficulty controlling his breathing and the fabric of his trousers was stretched tight. The image of him standing in front of Maggie as she fellated him flashed into Eleanor's mind, fuelling her desire. Her innate love of voyeurism no longer worried her; she had lost the sense of shame that had spoiled her enjoyment before. Now she used the images she had seen to stoke the fire of her passion.

She stood up and, holding Marcus's gaze, began to undress. Between her legs, her vulva, already sated by Tod in Cara's dungeon, felt heavy and moist. Her breasts also felt full and heavy, her nipples hardening in anticipation of his touch.

The one time they had come together it had been brief and savage, with no time to linger, or relish the giving and receiving of pleasure. This time she wanted it to last, to wring every last vestige of sensation out of him.

Marcus undressed too, in silence, the tension stretching between them, lengthening in the fading light of dusk. There was no tenderness in the way they looked at each other, no real feeling, just the swift, inexorable climb towards sexual frenzy. Eleanor didn't want tenderness. With a clear-mindedness that astounded her, she knew exactly what she wanted from him – passion.

To this end, she evaded him as he reached for

her, enclosing his erect cock in her hand instead and caressing it skilfully.

'Do you want me, Marcus?' she asked him, her voice low and husky.

'Isn't that obvious?'

'I want to hear you say it.'

She flicked her fingertips across the sensitive spot where his cock and scrotal sac met and his eyes momentarily closed.

'Yes, I want you, Eleanor,' he admitted through clenched teeth.

Eleanor leaned forward so that he could feel her warm breath brush his face.

'How much?' she whispered.

Marcus made a deep, primaeval sound, deep in his throat and his hand shot out to catch her at the back of her neck. Though she resisted for a moment, Eleanor knew at once that she was no match for his superior strength and she gave in gladly, lifting her face to his as he crushed her against him.

Letting go of his cock, she brought her arms up, around his neck as he kissed her, hard, grinding her lips against her teeth with a savagery which sent the adrenalin surging through her veins. Aware that what they were doing was closer to fighting than making love, Eleanor revelled in her new-found power to arouse.

Marcus's hands were hard as they moved urgently across her skin. His lips, as they moved from her mouth to her neck, were not gentle, nipping and sucking at her skin so that she shivered with growing excitement.

She felt so hot, as if she was glowing in the dusk, incandescent with desire. She let the feelings flow through her, no thought now of trying to control herself, or of suppressing her deepest, darkest desires. Following her instincts, she began to caress Marcus as he was her, pressing her lips against the tender place behind his ear before biting gently on the fleshy lobe.

As his fingers kneaded the softness of her breasts, so she raked her nails down his back, scoring the skin in her enthusiasm and making him suck in his breath.

'Jesus, Eleanor!' he gasped.

Clasping her head between his palms, he kissed her again, more urgently now, smothering her face with kisses as he manoeuvred her so that her back was against the cold plaster of the wall. Eleanor was barely aware of this small discomfort, she was swept along by the tide of his desire, completely caught up in the battle being enacted between them.

And it *was* a battle. Locked in an exclusive duel, neither wanting to concede to the other, they became steadily more frenzied. With Marcus's hard, lean body pressing her against the wall, Eleanor felt as if she couldn't breathe. Yet she revelled in the wholly masculine strength of him, welcoming the sensation of being overwhelmed, willing, in her mind at least, to submit to him.

186

Their eyes clashed and held, his dark and stormy, reflecting the tumult of emotion in hers. He didn't touch the melting place between her legs, merely lifting her with his hands at her waist and bringing her down on the strong shaft of his cock.

Eleanor moaned and brought her legs around his waist. Looking deep into her eyes, Marcus pressed her back against the wall and thrust into her, his fingers digging into the soft flesh of her waist. In response, Eleanor gripped him with her internal muscles, moving her hips so that after every savage thrust, she held onto him for a second longer than he wanted her to.

She could see from the look in his eyes that he was determined to maintain his formidable control, that he intended to triumph over her by making her come first. To this end, he shifted position slightly so that her pelvis was tipped forward. This meant that with every inward stroke, her clitoris was stroked by the slippery shaft of his penis, sending electric thrills of delight through to her womb.

Determined that he would not better her, Eleanor concentrated on milking him, squeezing rhythmically with her pelvic floor muscles until his breathing became rapid and his eyes began to glaze.

'How do you like what you've made of me, Marcus?' she whispered as the sweat broke out on the surface of his skin. 'How do you like a real, live, "retrained" woman enclosing you?'

'Eleanor . . .'

'You're going to come, Marcus. You're going to show me how much you appreciate the fruits of your research.'

'No . . .'

'Yes . . . oh yes!' She laughed softly as she saw his control slip away. 'Let it go, Marcus,' she murmured throatily.

Surreptitiously, she reached between them and pressed the pads of her fingers against the most sensitive spot at the base of his scrotum. Marcus's eyes opened wide and he regarded her with surprise as he was tipped over the edge.

'Yes . . . Eleanor . . . ahh!'

Eleanor wrapped herself around him as his orgasm broke, grinding her clitoris against his pubic bone to precipitate her own climax. Marcus sagged against her, and they slid down the wall together, still connected, still shuddering with the after-shocks of pleasure.

It was a few minutes before Marcus recovered. When he raised his head to look at her, there was a quiet fury in his eyes that sent a dark thrill along Eleanor's spine. He withdrew from her and they both lay on the floor, regarding each other warily.

'That felt more like anger than desire,' he said after a few minutes.

Eleanor flushed.

'Perhaps it was,' she admitted.

'Why?'

'Maybe I felt you needed teaching a lesson.'

'Teaching a lesson?'

'For your arrogance.'

Marcus shook his head.

'You're something else, you know that?' he said. 'It was your idea to use yourself as a test model – remember?'

'I remember.'

'Then don't turn on me because you regret it.'

'Regret it?' Eleanor laughed. 'I don't regret it, Marcus. But I'm not made of stone. I know what you've been doing.'

'Then perhaps you'd care to enlighten me?'

'As if you need enlightening!' Eleanor retorted, suppressed anger fuelling her words. 'You've teased and tested me until I didn't know whether I was on my head or my heels! Setting up my "research opportunities" whilst all the time pretending that you were nothing more than a scientist conducting an experiment!'

Marcus looked uncomfortable.

'I had to try to stay objective!' he said defensively.

'But you didn't, did you?' she taunted him. 'You wanted me, right from the start. But instead of being honest about it, you set me up so that you could watch and enjoy my responses without ever having to get involved yourself. It must have given you a shock that night when I pounced on you! How did it feel, Marcus, to be used as part of an experiment? Did you feel dehumanised? *Used?*

189

Did you, Marcus?'

'What's this really about, Eleanor?' he asked her quietly after a few minutes.

Eleanor stared at him, then, to her horror, she burst into tears. Marcus reached out to comfort her, but she turned her face away.

'No, damn you, I don't want your tenderness! Don't you understand? You've "trained" me to want sex, not affection. Goddammit, Marcus, I want you to make love to me!'

He waited until she had wiped her eyes on a tissue he passed her from the box on her bedside table.

'Make love to you?' he said.

'Yes. If it's not too much trouble!'

He smiled faintly.

'As opposed to fucking you?'

'That's right.'

'Okay. You only had to ask – we didn't have to go through that charade.'

Eleanor opened her mouth to protest that, had he wanted to make love to her, he wouldn't have waited for her to ask him, but she closed it again as she caught the look in his eye. Already, he was hardening again and she moved towards him.

'Shall we get up onto the bed?' he suggested. 'We'll be more comfortable there.'

He helped her up, then lowered her gently onto the covers. Eleanor felt herself relaxing, the restless, prickly feeling that had overcome her the first time conspicuous by its absence. Marcus kissed her, gently at first, then with more urgency. His hands were gentle on her body this time, stroking and caressing her, his fingers curling slowly into the hot, wet folds of her sex, seeking out her most sensitive places.

Cradling her head against his shoulder, he played her like a fine musical instrument, drawing out the pleasure until she felt like sobbing with the exquisite tension. When she came this time, it was with a rippling ecstasy, suffusing her with heat and making her want to stretch, like a cat, from head to toe.

Marcus lay back on the covers, watching her through half-closed eyes. Eleanor watched him in turn, knowing that, good though her climax had felt, there was something missing.

She reached for him, feeling him harden under her palm. The skin of his penis was smooth and velvety over the rigid core. Eleanor played her fingers up and down its length, watching his face for his reaction. A small pulse beat in his jaw as she cupped his balls with her hand and squeezed gently, brushing her fingernails across his perineum.

Seized by the same restlessness she had experienced earlier, she knelt up and straddled him, guiding the tip of his penis to the entrance to her body. Marcus looked at her expectantly, reaching up to caress her breasts as she sank down on him.

He filled her, his rigid shaft stretching the walls

of her vagina, knocking against her womb. Leaning back from the waist, she intensified the penetration, little shards of pain slicing through her, making her lean towards him again. Slowly, she began to ride him, lifting herself up to the point where it felt as though he would slip out of her before sinking back down again, enclosing him.

Beads of perspiration filmed his upper lip and Eleanor dipped her head to dab at them with her tongue. Marcus held her close, rising up so that they were sitting facing each other, joined at the centre. They rocked back and forth, he barely moving at all inside her, yet setting up a vibration that seemed to travel through her, even along her limbs.

They kissed, urgently, deeply, and Eleanor felt his climax pulse along his cock before he shuddered convulsively, and came. Gazing into his eyes, she saw that he was sated, satisfied with their encounter. And at that moment Eleanor knew, with utmost certainty, that she was not. Passionate though it had been, though his technique was, technically, as close to perfection as she guessed it was possible to get, there was still something missing. And whatever that elusive something was, it was central to her happiness.

'What are you doing?'

Eleanor turned to find Marcus watching her from the doorway of her study. His expression was wary and she sighed inwardly. How could she

192

explain something that she didn't understand herself?

'I'm going home,' she told him.

'Before the end of the project? Isn't this a bit sudden?'

She shrugged.

'Perhaps, in one way. I'm not reneging on my part of the deal, Marcus, I just feel that it would be better if I write the concluding chapters away from here. I need to distance myself from you, and your side of the project.'

'Why?'

'Call it an intuitive whim.'

Marcus stepped inside the room, his expression thoughtful.

'I thought last night was . . . good,' he said, a note of caution apparent in his voice.

'It *was* good, Marcus. But I need to get away.'

'All right. But so soon? Won't you stay another night at least, talk it over?'

Eleanor shook her head.

'No, my mind is made up. I've learned all I needed to learn. The research is over, my education complete. Last night was my graduation, if you like. Now I need space to draw my conclusions.'

She thought, for a moment, that he would continue to try to dissuade her from the course she had chosen, but he lifted his hands in a small gesture of helplessness.

'Okay. I guess I can telephone and fax you in the

Valleys?'

'Of course.'

He nodded, flashing her a small smile.

'I fly back to the States on the thirtieth.'

'I'll send you the manuscript in good time.'

'Nothing I can say will persuade you to stay?'

Eleanor thought of the peace of her home and shook her head.

'Then I wish you a safe journey, until we meet again.'

'Thank you, Marcus.'

Eleanor kissed him impulsively on the cheek then, overcome by a sudden, urgent desire to be on her way, she picked up her bags and walked quickly out of the door. She could sense his all-seeing, all-knowing gaze on her even after the door swung closed behind her. But she did not look back, not once.

# Chapter Ten

---

*LOOKING OUT OF* the window of the train taking her home, Eleanor marvelled at how everything looked the same. Such momentous changes had occured within her over the few short weeks of her absence, she almost expected the lush, green fields to be sparkling with diamond-bright dew, for rainbows to criss-cross the sky.

She smiled to herself at the fancy. In truth, she did see things differently, though in more subtle ways. Colours seemed to be sharper, flavours more defined, she was more attuned to everything around her. It was as if she had spent her life with her head inside a paper bag, never really noticing what went on around her. A period of looking inward, of being deliberately self-obsessed, seemed to have sharpened her perceptions generally.

Rhys was waiting for her at the station. He was

wearing old jeans and a faded rugby shirt and his hair was tousled by the wind blowing along the platform. Eleanor thought she had never seen him look more handsome and she felt her spirits lift, her heart turning a little somersault as she caught sight of him, and she hurried to get out of the train.

'I didn't expect to see you!' she said.

Moving into his arms seemed like the most natural thing in the world. He looked a little taken aback by the unrestrained warmth of her greeting, but his arms came about her without hesitation and he kissed her upturned face with unconcealed affection.

'Welcome home, *cariad*,' he said gruffly.

Eleanor gazed up at him and realised, with a jolt, that 'home' was here, in his arms. She hadn't realised quite how much she had been looking forward to seeing him, how much she had hoped that her 'casual' mention on the phone that she would be arriving on this train would prompt him to meet her.

'Are you free for the rest of the day?' she asked him as he picked up her bags and walked with her along the concourse.

'I'm on leave until Tuesday next,' he told her, 'so I can drive you all the way home, if that's what you were thinking.'

Eleanor laughed softly.

'Actually, I was wondering if you might be able to stay. If you'd like to, that is,' she added hastily, struck by a sudden, inconvenient shyness.

Rhys stopped walking and turned to look at her.

'Do you mean what I think you mean, Eleanor?' he asked her, his eyes scanning her features as if hoping to find the answers to all his questions in her face.

Eleanor reached up to trace the rugged outline of his cheek with her fingertips. She knew that she was looking at him with love in her eyes, and that he would know how she felt.

'Yes,' she answered, 'I'm ready now.'

Rhys didn't say a word, though his pupils dilated and his jaw tightened as he took her by the hand and they began walking again.

There was a tension between them in the car, but it did not cause an unpleasant atmosphere. Emboldened by her own feelings, Eleanor leaned her head lightly on his shoulder as he drove, confident that she would soon be able to express the way she felt about him in a way that would convince him once and for all.

Poor Rhys – he had had to wait for so long! Yet she knew now that there had been a purpose to his long vigil, that she had needed to find herself before she was ready to share her life with him. She had to learn to love herself before she could be ready to allow someone else to love her.

At the cottage, Dylan and Thomas greeted her with typical feline disdain and stalked past her without so much as a glance. The house felt unlived in and they went around throwing all the windows open wide to allow the fragrant sea air to waft through.

They met on the landing, each of them stopping on either side of the stairwell as if caught unawares by the presence of the other. Eleanor sensed the tension in him as he waited for her to speak and knew that what happened now would affect her always.

She smiled, stepping forward out of the shadows to take him by the hand.

'Love me, Rhys,' she said softly.

'Always,' he murmured in response, walking with her into the small, oak-beamed bedroom.

He dwarfed the room by his presence, having to dip his head as she led him over to the ancient bed beneath the sloping roof. Eleanor turned and smiled at him, aware of an inward trembling that had nothing to do with desire and everything to do with the fear that it wouldn't live up to her expectations. Having conditioned herself to climb the sexual heights, what would she do if making love with Rhys was dull? Or – oh Lord, don't let it happen – if he rejected her now?

She needn't have worried. Such thoughts flew from her mind as he reached out and traced the outline of her cheek with his forefinger, before cupping her face with his hand. Eleanor turned her head and kissed the warm, dry creases of his palm and he responded by brushing his thumbpad across her lips.

All his attention seemed to be focused on her

mouth as he caressed the soft, fleshy inner surface of her bottom lip. Eleanor could sense the tension building in him, and knew instinctively that he was as nervous of beginning this as she was. They had both waited so long that they were afraid that the reality might not live up to the expectation.

There was only one way to find out. Trembling, Eleanor touched his face, brushing her fingertips lightly over his lips and closing the small gap which was still between them. Rhys sighed, a yearning, ragged sound, then he put his arms around her and touched his lips against hers.

It was like setting light to touchpaper. Desire rose up between them like a flame, rapidly turning into a conflagration as the kiss deepened and they clung together. Eleanor barely noticed that they had moved until she felt the edge of the bed behind her knees, then Rhys was lowering her slowly onto it, his firm, hard body covering her, imprinting its shape onto the softness of hers.

She was conscious of the unique scent of his skin as she pressed her face against his neck as he removed his weight from her. It was a fresh, woody smell, wholly masculine, and she breathed it in deeply. Then the sensations of sight, sound, smell and taste merged into a blur, subjugated to the pressing need to touch and be touched.

Rhys helped her out of her clothes, pausing every few seconds to kiss and touch the warm flesh he had uncovered. Though she was conscious of a sense of urgency, Rhys was clearly in no hurry, wanting instead to savour every moment of this long-awaited first time together.

He smiled at her when she finally lay naked on the covers and there was such a tenderness in that smile that Eleanor felt unexpected tears brim in her eyes.

'What is it, *cariad*?' he asked, his eyes darkening with concern.

'Nothing,' she whispered. 'Only that . . . I never thought this would happen between us.'

'If you're having second thoughts—'

'I'm not,' she interrupted him, pressing the tips of her fingers against his lips to silence him.

'Good. Because after tonight, Eleanor, we will belong together you and I, just as we always have, but bound by something far more sacred.'

Eleanor gazed at him, awed by the solemnity of his expression and the feeling behind his words. He was looking at her expectantly, as if holding back until she had given him some sign of commitment. She felt herself smiling, wanting to express the joy she felt.

'I know. Make love to me, Rhys.'

He smiled again, only this time there was something about the way he looked at her that sent a shiver along her spine. There was an intensity in the depths of his eyes that set a small pulse beating at the centre of her.

Rhys held up his hand and Eleanor touched his

spread fingertips with hers. The warmth of his skin seemed to spread through her fingers, into her hand and down her arms. Slowly, their fingers entwined, their hands meshing as if one hand, and Rhys held it against his heart. He didn't need to say anything, she could feel his heart thudding in his chest, strong and regular, but a little faster than normal, and she knew that he felt the same way as she did, that he wanted her just as much as she wanted him.

He lowered his head, so slowly, to place a kiss on the tip of one breast. The nipple responded instantly to the tiny caress, hardening and drawing into a small peak of need. Eleanor moaned softly as Rhys teased it with his tongue before, taking pity on her, he drew the aching nub into the warm, wet cavity of his mouth.

Eleanor tangled her fingers in his hair, holding his head against her breast as he pulled it deeper into his mouth. Her womb cramped with longing as he sucked, the sensitive folds of flesh between her thighs swelling and moistening in direct response.

'Oh, Rhys,' she whispered, her voice shuddering.

His hands were at her waist, smoothing the skin, sending little ripples of delight along her nerve endings. She moaned in protest when he levered himself away from her, until she realised that it was only to enable him to remove his clothes.

Eleanor watched through narrowed eyes as he undressed, taking a voyeuristic pleasure in looking at him. His shoulders were broad, the muscles of his upper arms bulging as he pulled his shirt over his head. There was a fine smattering of blond hair on his chest, but his skin was smooth and velvety over the steel of his pecs, his nipples pale and flat.

'You look like you work out,' she commented, reaching out a hand to trace the definition of his stomach muscles. They contracted under her palm as she inched her hand lower to the fastening of his jeans and she smiled wickedly at him. 'Let me take these off.'

Rhys said nothing, but Eleanor could tell by the way he held himself, so still, as if afraid of breaking the moment, that he wanted her to undress him. Standing at the side of the bed, he held himself rigid as Eleanor slipped the buttons through the buttonholes on his fly front and eased the stiff denim smoothly over his hips.

Underneath, he was wearing plain white jersey boxer shorts which clung to the outline of his erection, delineating it lovingly. Eleanor pressed her cheek gently against the length of him, making him tremble, before peeling the briefs down, over his taut buttocks and down his thighs.

His cock was strong and straight, the circumcised tip smooth and pink. As she watched, a tear of fluid streaked the neat slit and she dabbed at it with her tongue, absorbing Rhys's deep sigh of pleasure.

'Eleanor—' he began, whatever he was about to say cut off by the shock of having her lips enclosing the bulbous head of his penis.

She drew him deeply into her mouth, relishing the taste and texture of him, wanting to show him how much she loved him. Rhys stood very still, careful not to give in to the instinct to thrust his hips forward and force himself further inside her mouth. Eleanor was aware that his breathing had grown shallow. His fingers caressed her hair and he murmured ragged endearments as she flicked her tongue along the underside of his cock.

Reaching beneath him, Eleanor stroked the taut, hair-roughened sacs at the base of his penis, pressing gently against the seam.

'Eleanor – wait!' Rhys cupped her jaw with his hands as he withdrew from her.

Eleanor looked up at him quizzically, through her lashes.

'Not yet,' he said softly. 'We've got all night . . . let me look at you.'

He pushed her gently onto her back, one hand reaching beneath her to cup her buttocks, his fingers pressing softly into the crease between them. Eleanor bent her legs at the knees as he tipped her pelvis up, exposing her most intimate flesh to his loving gaze.

Eleanor knew that she was swollen and moist, that the plump, slippery folds of flesh would be a dark rose pink, suffused with blood. There would be no mistaking the extent of her arousal, no doubt how much she wanted him now. She was proud that her body had responded so readily to him.

'So beautiful, *cariad*,' Rhys breathed, his fingers stroking lovingly along the open channels of flesh.

Eleanor shivered and reached for him, wanting to feel his mouth against hers as he pleasured her. They kissed, deeply, tongues caressing, lips nipping and sucking, drawing the sweetness from each other. Eleanor drew away, arching her neck and closing her eyes as the first shards of sensation pierced her. Rhys moved her clitoris, instinctively knowing how much pressure to apply and how fast to move his fingers. He leaned over her, watching her face as she came.

As she opened her eyes, she found herself staring straight into his eyes. He held her gaze as he eased her legs apart and touched his cock against the stretched membranes of her vulva. There was a question in his eyes which she answered gladly by reaching round to place her palms on the taut planes of his buttocks.

He eased into her, inch by inch, so that she was aware of her vaginal walls stretching to accommodate him, her muscles contracting to draw him in further. Rhys's eyes glazed over as he began to move inside her, and Eleanor knew that, this time, it would not take long for him to come.

She was right. He gasped her name as his seed surged along his shaft and Eleanor clung to him, revelling in the way he had given himself to her, wholeheartedly, without holding any part of him back.

'Oh Eleanor,' he whispered when, at last, it was over.

She smiled at him and laid her head against the tender cup of his shoulder. Five minutes, she decided. That's how long she would give him to recover . . .

This time, with the first urgent need assuaged, Eleanor was happy to take her time, to discover as much about him as she could. Rhys lay back and let her explore his body with her fingertips, lips and tongue, until she felt she knew every part of him, and he was hard again, his cock rearing up from his groin like a sentinel, as potent as ever.

Eleanor felt no need for foreplay, she merely straddled him and sank down on his cock. Once he was inside her, she sat very still, enjoying for the moment the simple sensation of him filling her. Their eyes met and held and Eleanor surprised an expression in his that she couldn't quite interpret.

'What?' she said, 'What is it?'

Smiling, Rhys reached up to hold her at the waist.

'I was thinking how magnificent you look, sitting there like that. I always thought you were the woman for me, Eleanor – now I know it. Without the slightest doubt, I know it.'

205

Before she realised his intention, Rhys flipped her over so that he was on top of her, then, to her dismay, he withdrew.

'Roll over,' he said.

Eleanor responded to the gruff note of command in his voice with a thrill of delight. Only briefly did she recall that this was how Michael had always taken her. Aware that Rhys had breached her final taboo, Eleanor sighed as he sank into her, raising her hips to ease his path.

Folding his body over hers, Rhys held her, one hand balancing his own weight, the other splaying across her pubis, the middle finger finding her clitoris. Eleanor felt it reawaken under his touch, a small pulse throbbing deep inside her.

Turning her head, she found his mouth and kissed him. She came, seconds before he did, the convulsions of her inner sex triggering his own climax. Collapsing in a tangle of sweaty limbs, they curled together under the covers, laughing as they stuck together. Rhys cradled Eleanor in his arms and she pressed her lips against the thud of his heartbeat. Within minutes, they both fell asleep.

The path to *Becoming Sexual* will be a different one for each and every woman, a personal odyssey that only the woman herself can prescribe. Each of us must find our own way to shangri-la. To do so we have to learn to trust our own instincts, to know that we are the best judge of what is right for us.

There is only so much that can be learned from books and videos and the sex gurus of our times. There is no real substitute for personal experience. The main use of a book such as this is to spread the word that it *is* possible to 'retrain' ones learned sexual response, that the ability to unlock our true sexual potential is there in each and every one of us.

As women, we owe it to ourselves to discover the extent of our propensity for pleasure. It doesn't matter how long it has been locked away, it *can* be released, but only *you* can set it free.

Equally, only you can decide what to do with it once it is found. Sex is a wonderful thing, the sharing of pleasures a profound and enduring delight. Yet I have come to realise in the course of my research for this book that sex, in itself, is not enough.


Eleanor paused, aware that this was the message she needed to get across to Marcus, that if she could make him understand this, he would understand, finally, everything that had happened during the writing of the book.

She wanted him to understand, and perhaps to look inside his own heart and realise what she felt was missing in his life. Willing the right words to come, Eleanor sat, fingers poised above the keyboard.

Love is the key. Without love the physical act is meaningless, a soul-less transaction between strangers. Yes, it is possible to 'become sexual' in the ways described in this book, it is possible to 'train' the mind and body to recognise certain stimuli and to react accordingly. But only when there is love between the two people involved can the physical act of sex transcend the mechanical and transport the participants to a plane of pure bliss.

Once on that plane, it is possible to realise that the true joy of becoming sexual is not for its own sake, but for the deepening of a loving relationship. The search for love will always be the nobler pursuit, for without it, there will always be something missing.

'Eleanor?'

She turned to see Rhys was awake, gazing at her through sleep-glazed eyes as if surprised to see her there.

'What are you doing?'

Eleanor smiled at him.

'Just finishing my part of the book. Don't worry – go back to sleep.'

'Alone?' he said, smiling wolfishly at her.

Eleanor shook her head with mock exasperation.

'Rhys Wynn-Jones, you are insatiable!'

He watched her as she stood and unfastened her robe, letting it fall to the ground. Holding his eyes, she slipped beneath the covers and slid luxuriously into the warmth of his embrace, knowing that it could only bring her joy.

# Epilogue

RHYS NEVER DID find out the part Eleanor played in the writing of *Becoming Sexual*. Even when the book caused a stir and media speculation was rife about the female guinea-pig described, he never seemed to connect the character with Eleanor. Or so she thought.

Eighteen months later she received a Jiffy bag from the States containing a copy of the American version of Marcus's next book. Opening it, she raised her eyebrows at the title.

*In Search of Love*.

Flicking through the pages, she realised that, this time, Marcus had used himself as his research tool, acting on the conclusions that Eleanor had drawn at the end of their joint project. Turning to the flyleaf, Eleanor saw that there was a printed dedication there.

*To Eleanor*, she read, *without whom this book*

*would never have been conceived.*

Underneath it, Marcus had written in his bold, neat handwriting, *You were right, and I was wrong – thank you!*

There was an envelope tucked into the pages addressed to Mr and Mrs R. Wynn-Jones. Curious, Eleanor slit it open and drew out the single white card inside. It was a wedding invitation.

'So he listened to you, then?'

Eleanor jumped as Rhys came up behind her silently and slipped his arms around her waist. His hands rested comfortably on the growing bulge at her waistline and Eleanor leaned into him automatically.

'You knew?' she said, the significance of what he had said only just hitting her.

'Of course.' There was a smile in his voice which dissipated some of the nervousness that had seized her when she realised that he had known all along about the part she had played in Marcus's last book.

'But you never said . . .'

'You'd have told me, if you wanted me to know.'

He kissed her hair and Eleanor closed her eyes for a moment, breathing in the dear, familiar scent of him.

'And you don't mind?'

Rhys turned her in his arms and she saw that his expression was serious.

'Eleanor,' he said, 'whatever it took – all that matters to me is that it brought you back home to me.'

Eleanor gazed at him, her heart filling with love as it did every time she looked at him. To be so well loved still amazed and overwhelmed her. She hoped that she never lost the wonder of it.

'Marcus has invited us to his wedding,' she told him.

'So he found love.'

'Apparently.'

Rhys scanned her face.

'What do you think of when you think of him?'

Eleanor could feel a blush stealing into her cheeks. Aware that Rhys was watching her closely, she knew that nothing but total honesty would do.

'I feel . . . warmly towards him, I suppose. I'm glad he's found someone. And no, before you ask, I would never have wanted it to be me.'

Rhys smiled and his face seemed to clear.

'When is the wedding?' he asked her.

Glancing at the invitation, Eleanor saw that it was scheduled to take place in California, in June.

'It'll be too close,' she said, laying a hand protectively on their unborn child.

'Perhaps it's just as well.'

'Oh?'

Rhys shrugged, a small, self-deprecating gesture that tugged at her heartstrings.

'I do understand, honestly, *cariad*. But I'm only flesh and blood – I don't really want to meet him.'

Eleanor smiled and moved into his arms.

'I'll write,' she said, 'to wish them well.'

Rhys nodded and touched his lips against hers.

'If they have half the happiness that we have—'

'I know. I think Marcus has learned as much from me as I did from him.'

'We won't speak of it again, then,' Rhys said, his lips brushing softly against hers.

'No,' she agreed. 'It was only a brief moment in time. You and I have our whole lives to look forward to together.'

'Yes, *cariad* – together,' Rhys echoed as his mouth claimed hers for his own.

# BACK IN CHARGE
**Mariah Greene**

A woman in control. Sexy, successful, sure of herself and of what she wants, Andrea King is an ambitious account handler in a top advertising agency. Life seems sweet, as she heads for promotion and enjoys the attentions of her virile young boyfriend.

But strange things are afoot at the agency. A shake-up is ordered, with the key job of Creative Director in the balance. Andrea has her rivals for the post, but when the chance of winning a major new account presents itself, she will go to any lengths to please her client – and herself . . .

0 7515 1276 1

# THE DISCIPLINE OF PEARLS
**Susan Swann**

A mysterious gift, handed to her by a dark and arrogant stranger. Who was he? How did he know so much about her? How did he know her life was crying out for something different? Something . . . exciting, erotic?

The pearl pendant, and the accompanying card bearing an unknown telephone number, propel Marika into a world of uninhibited sexuality, filled with the promise of a desire she had never thought possible. The Discipline of Pearls . . . an exclusive society that speaks to the very core of her sexual being, bringing with it calls to ecstasies she is powerless to ignore, unwilling to resist . . .

0 7515 1277 X

## HOTEL APHRODISIA
## Dorothy Starr

The luxury hotel of Bouvier Manor nestles near a spring whose mineral water is reputed to have powerful aphrodisiac qualities. Whether this is true or not, Dani Stratton, the hotel's feisty receptionist, finds concentrating on work rather tricky, particularly when the muscularly attractive Mitch is around.

And even as a mysterious consortium threatens to take over the Manor, staff and guests seem quite unable to control their insatiable thirsts . . .

0 7515 1287 7


## AROUSING ANNA
## Nina Sheridan

Anna had always assumed she was frigid. At least, that's what her husband Paul had always told her – in between telling her to keep still during their weekly fumblings under the covers and playing the field himself during his many business trips.

But one such trip provides the chance that Anna didn't even know she was yearning for. Agreeing to put up a lecturer who is visiting the university where she works, she expects to be host to a dry, elderly academic, and certainly isn't expecting a dashing young Frenchman who immediately speaks to her innermost desires. And, much to her delight and surprise, the vibrant Dominic proves himself able and willing to apply himself to the task of arousing Anna . . .

0 7515 1222 2

# THE WOMEN'S CLUB
## Vanessa Davies

*Sybarites* is a health club with a difference. Its owner, Julia Marquis, has introduced a full range of services to guarantee complete satisfaction. For after their saunas and facials the exclusively female members can enjoy an 'intimate' massage from one of the club's expert masseurs.

And now, with the arrival of Grant Delaney, it seems the privileged clientele of the women's club will be getting even better value for their money. This talented masseur can fulfil any woman's erotic dreams.

Except Julia's . . .

0 7515 1343 1


# PLAYING THE GAME
## Selina Seymour

Kate has had enough. No longer is she prepared to pander to the whims of lovers who don't love her; no longer will she cater for their desires while neglecting her own.

But in reaching this decision Kate makes a startling discovery: the potency of her sexual urge, now given free rein through her willingness to play men at their own game. And it is an urge that doesn't go unnoticed – whether at her chauvinistic City firm, at the château of a new French client, or in performing the duties of a high-class call girl . . .

0 7515 1189 7

## A SLAVE TO HIS KISS
**Anastasia Dubois**

When her twin sister Cassie goes missing in the South of France, Venetia Fellowes knows she must do everything in her power to find her. But in the dusty village of Valazur, where Cassie was last seen, a strange aura of complicity connects those who knew her, heightened by an atmosphere of unrestrained sexuality.

As her fears for Cassie's safety mount, Venetia turns to the one person who might be able to help: the enigmatic Esteban, a study in sexual mystery whose powerful spell demands the ultimate sacrifice . . .

0 7515 1344 X

## SATURNALIA
**Zara Devereux**

Recently widowed, Heather Logan is concerned about her sex-life. Even when married it was plainly unsatisfactory, and now the prospects for sexual fulfilment look decidedly thin.

After consulting a worldly friend, however, Heather takes his advice and checks in to Tostavyn Grange, a private hotel-cum-therapy centre for sexual inhibition. Heather had been warned about their 'unconventional' methods, but after the preliminary session, in which she is brought to a thunderous climax – her first – she is more than willing to complete the course . . .

0 7515 1342 3